POOL BOYS

POOL BOYS

ERIN HAFT

SCHOLASTIC INC.
New York   Toronto   London   Auckland   Sydney
Mexico City   New Delhi   Hong Kong   Buenos Aires

ISBN 0-439-83523-2

Copyright © 2006 by Erin Haft

SCHOLASTIC and associated logos are trademarks and/or registered trademarks of Scholastic Inc.

Text design by Steve Scott.
Text type was set in Sabon.

12 11 10 9 8 7 6 5 4 3 2   6 7 8 9 10 11/0

Printed in the U.S.A.
First Scholastic printing, May 2006

For Aimee Friedman,
who knows just how to
dive in and make a big splash

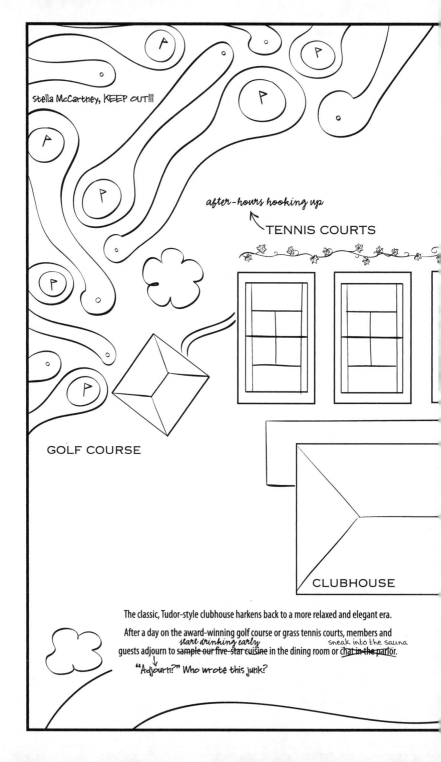

Stella McCartney, KEEP OUT!!!

after-hours hooking up

TENNIS COURTS

GOLF COURSE

CLUBHOUSE

The classic, Tudor-style clubhouse harkens back to a more relaxed and elegant era.

After a day on the award-winning golf course or grass tennis courts, members and
guests adjourn to sample our five-star cuisine in the dining room or chat in the parlor.

start drinking early

sneak into the sauna

"Adjourn?" Who wrote this junk?

Silver S O *Oaks*
COUNTRY CLUB

Established in 1922, The Silver Oaks Country Club represents a heritage of comfort, ~~service~~, and extra-marital affairs
refined ambiance. Throughout our ~~proud~~ history, we have sought to uphold the genteel values *sketchy*
of the original founders, who placed a premium on making/their guests ~~feel welcome~~. *out with*

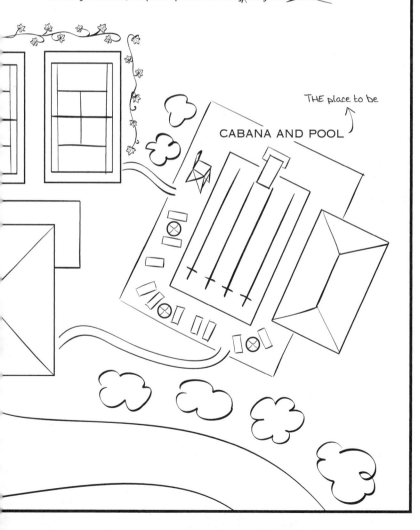

THE place to be

CABANA AND POOL

The Silver Oaks Country Club
~ A FAMILY INSTITUTION ~

Rules:

Members will treat fellow members with respect and decorum.

Members will not engage socially with staff.

Members will not smoke on the premises.

Members will leave their pets at home.

Members will not gamble or place any unapproved wagers while on the premises.

Members will wear approved footgear at all times in the dining room.

UNSPOKEN RULES: (By Brooke, Charlotte, and Georgia)

1. Never Underestimate an Entrance.

2. Thou Shalt Not Poach Thy Friend's Love Interest.

3. Sportsmanship, Schmortsmanship...

4. In Case of Rain, Please Convene in the Billiards Room to Watch the Pool Boys Make Jackasses of Themselves, Trying to Play "Pool."

5. I forget.

6. Don't Toss Out Anything of Value. Also Stay Away from the Cabana After Certain People Have Used It.

Chapter One

The First Unspoken Rule

"You guys?" Brooke Farnsworth whispered to her two best friends. "I've seen the future, and his name is Marcus Craft. I told you this summer would be killer, didn't I?"

Brooke huddled with Georgia Palmer and Charlotte von Klaus in the shadows of the cabana entrance, surveying the otherwise deserted pool patio in the bright June morning. There was still a chill in the air — in coastal Connecticut, summer never truly kicked in until July — and she shivered, partly from the breeze, and partly from delight.

Brooke glanced back inside at the terry-cloth robes hanging near the door, freshly washed and waiting, the silver *S.O.* monograms glinting on each lapel. (Every item of white cloth on the premises of the Silver Oaks Country Club bore the same stitched silver monogram, from the napkins in the dining room to the curtains in the parlor.) Maybe she and Georgia and Charlotte should have worn robes over their bikinis? Nah. . . .

Brooke turned back toward the pool. It was all just as she remembered from last June: the piles of fluffy towels, the empty loungers, the water like a solid block of blue ice.

Everything that symbolized the start of another typical Silver Oaks season ... everything that is, except for the shaggy blond boy in the lifeguard chair.

"I thought you said this summer would be more of the same old, same old," Georgia teased.

"Did I?" Brooke whispered back. "Please stop listening to anything I say at school."

"Let's just hope he can swim," Charlotte muttered.

The three girls broke into laughter, but Brooke quickly brought a hand to her glossy lips. She didn't want Marcus Craft to notice her. Not quite yet. She wanted him to spy her as she strolled over and settled into her usual lounger at the far edge of the patio, the one under the big green umbrella, right next to the ivy-covered fence adjoining the tennis courts. Brooke had been settling into that lounger for as long as she'd been wearing a bikini, and she'd learned how to play it for its full effect.

Brooke was obsessed with entrances.

"Is he looking at me?" Brooke whispered. She brushed a lone strand of shiny black hair out of her hazel eyes, then pulled a tube of sunblock out of her fringed Botkia bag, squeezing a dollop of cream on her shoulders. Thankfully, Marcus was too far away to read the SPF 45 label.

Charlotte snickered.

"What?" Brooke said.

"Yes, he's looking at you," Georgia groaned. "Who else would he look at?"

"Sweetie, you're the one who's tall, blonde, and gorgeous." Brooke raised her eyebrows at Georgia over her new Marc Jacobs sunglasses. (Props to Mom for the shades: In spite of the woman's fiendishness, Theresa Farnsworth always came through with the perfect end-of-school-year present.) "And, as far as males are concerned, tall, blonde, and gorgeous trumps short, black-haired, and pale every day of the week."

"You're *raven*-haired," Charlotte chided. "You have to remember that, B. You're not pale; you're porcelain. You're not short; you're petite. Just like I'm *not* an Orphan Annie clone." Charlotte flipped her long red curls over her shoulder and struck an exaggeratedly seductive pose. "I'm a fiery she-demon. Have I taught you nothing?"

"You did once, I think," Brooke said dryly. She tucked the sunblock back in her bag. "You taught me how to pad my bra. In the cabana, the summer after seventh grade."

"I think you taught me that, too," Georgia told Charlotte.

"I think I taught me that, three," Charlotte added.

They laughed again, and Brooke glanced toward the lifeguard chair. Remarkably, Marcus *was* looking at her. She felt a tingle of anticipation.

"Hey, Marcus!" Charlotte called suddenly, stepping into the sunshine and waving up to him, high on his lonely perch over the pool. "It's Marcus, isn't it? I'm Charlotte, and this is Brooke and Georgia. We know everything there is to know about Silver Oaks — especially the bad stuff. So if you have any questions — you know, questions about things you don't want to ask anyone else — feel free to ask us."

And thank you, C, for stealing my entrance, Brooke thought with a smirk.

"Uh . . . okay," Marcus called back. He flashed a puzzled grin, his blue eyes roving over the three of them. Clearly, he had no idea what Charlotte was talking about. But then, few people other than Georgia or Brooke *ever* knew what Charlotte von Klaus was talking about. "Thanks. Nice to meet you."

"The pleasure's all ours," Charlotte replied under her breath.

Brooke suppressed a smile as she trailed Charlotte and Georgia across the flagstones toward the opposite side of the pool, their flip-flops slapping in an uneven rhythm. She couldn't help but steal another peek at the lifeguard. Marcus's presence was a sign. Definitely. How could it not be? It wasn't just that she and Charlotte and Georgia were the first to arrive at the pool — per tradition, of course — on the first day of the new season, and therefore the first to spot this new boy. It wasn't even that he was ridiculously hot, with the square jaw, the blond mane, and the cocoa tan. . . .

It was that he was new.

The last handsome new employee at Silver Oaks had been Ethan Brennan, the twenty-year-old tennis instructor. And that had been two years ago. Plus, Ethan wasn't hot; he was cute (there *is* a difference) in a sort of crunchy slacker way. And, as a junior at the local community college, he also seemed content to spend the rest of his life at Silver Oaks. Which was fine. But it meant that thirty years from now, he'd still be giving tennis lessons and roaming the grounds making wisecracks, while Brooke, Georgia, and Charlotte discussed their kids' outrageous college tuition.

Not that Brooke would ever have said any of this out loud. Georgia had briefly dated Ethan last summer, in a rare and direct violation of the Spoken Rules. Worse, Brooke knew Georgia was still wrestling with some lingering feelings for him. But that was a whole other can of worms not worth opening. Ethan Brennan was old news. Brooke could already tell that Marcus was different. How perfect was it that he was a lifeguard? With white sunscreen on his nose, no less! They used to make cheesy *movies* about lifeguards with white sunscreen. One rainy afternoon last summer, after a few G&Ts, Mrs. Farnsworth had forced Brooke and Georgia and Charlotte to watch a "Beach Blanket" movie marathon, starring some horrible-haired guy named Frankie Avalon. (The pastel bathing suits were classic, though. Why were older generations so afraid of showing skin?) A romance with a new lifeguard was a tradition. Or, rather, it *should* have been at a country club like Silver Oaks. Brooke practically owed it to herself to try it out.

"I can't *believe* I said this summer was going to be more of the same old, same old," she murmured. She kicked off her flip-flops and stretched out her legs, sinking into the lounger's familiar white cushions — all the while pretending to be oblivious to the possibility that Marcus was still staring at her. "I am an idiot."

"Brooke, you shouldn't confess so much out in the open," a gravelly male voice announced.

She sat up and turned around. *Speak of the devil.* Ethan Brennan stood on the other side of the fence, his curly brown hair tousled. He clutched his racket in one hand, trying to clear away the ivy with the other. Not surprisingly, his Silver Oaks–issued tennis whites were a little rumpled and less than white.

"Hey there, Mr. Tennis Pro," Brooke said. "I was just thinking about you."

"That's funny, I was just thinking about me, too," he replied with a lazy smile.

By the looks of his jawline, he hadn't shaved in several days. But that was Ethan. He wasn't trying to cultivate a scruffy image; he'd probably just forgotten. Fortunately for him, he was just sexy enough to get away with scruff.

"Don't you know better than to listen in on ladies' conversations, Ethan?" Charlotte quipped, settling into the lounger beside Brooke.

Grinning, Ethan swatted a stray vine out of his face and hung on to the chain-link fence with his other hand. "I can't help it. I get high on eavesdropping. And on trying to scrounge a decent tennis game before the dinosaurs arrive — oops! I mean your parents. G, what do you say to a quick set?"

"I . . . well, I'm in my bikini," Georgia stammered. She stood awkwardly, fiddling with her towel. "I'd have to change."

"Come on. It'll be fun. We haven't played in so long. Seriously. I'm desperate for a good game."

Georgia glanced at Brooke and Charlotte. The message in her anxious, dark-blue eyes was plain: *Please help make up an excuse for me, you guys. He still calls me "G." He still jokes around with me. It's still too weird, even after all this time.*

For reasons Brooke couldn't fathom, Ethan had insisted on remaining friends with Georgia after their breakup. Brooke knew that Georgia wanted to get over him and get on with her life. But there was one problem: She was too nice to blow him off. Brooke had known Georgia her whole life, and couldn't remember her friend saying a mean thing about anyone, *ever*. She'd been displeased with people, sure: her parents, Ethan, even Brooke and Charlotte every now and then . . . but she always kept her angst to herself. One day that girl was going to burst.

"We just got here, Ethan," Brooke piped up. "Besides, you won't have to wait long for a game. My mom is changing into her new tennis whites as we speak. She spent all of May shopping for the perfect outfit: a conservative version of Venus Williams's minidresses. You'll be proud. But the three of us have to catch up. You know, girl stuff."

He chuckled. "Girl stuff? You guys talk to each other every single day. You go to the same school, don't you?" His eyes drifted over to the pool. "Hey, have you met the new girl yet? She seems really cool."

"What new girl?" all three girls asked at the same time. Brooke turned. "Where . . . ?" Her voice trailed off.

A tall, cheap-looking blonde had appeared out of nowhere — in a black Versace bikini. *The exact same one Brooke was wearing.* And now she was standing in front of the lifeguard chair, shaking hands with Marcus Craft. And he was trying not to stare at her chest. And . . . okay, she wasn't so cheap-looking. Far from it. She was Georgia's height, but skinnier — with flawless skin and a cascade of curls that rivaled Charlotte's. Except *her* curls were golden, like Cinderella's.

This was not good. Miss Thing had not only stolen Brooke's bathing suit (unintentionally, but still), she'd made contact with the guy Brooke had spotted first. How had *that* happened? She didn't belong here. Not this early, on the first day of the season. This was Brooke and Georgia and Charlotte's time. *And look at how she's flirting*, Brooke fumed. She and Marcus Craft were already making chit-chat, like a couple of newly partnered models preparing for a *Vogue* spread. Obviously, the new girl, whoever she was, had figured out the First Unspoken Rule. And she'd made her entrance right under Brooke's nose.

". . . name is Valerie," Ethan was saying. "She just moved here from New York. Her parents are friends with the Millers. I wonder if *she* plays tennis."

"Valerie, huh?" Charlotte mumbled. "She's pretty."

"She's really pretty," Georgia agreed, sounding depressed.

"Please," Brooke said dismissively, readjusting her

shades. She settled back into the lounger with a sigh. "You're both a thousand times hotter."

"Ha!" Ethan laughed.

Brooke frowned. "What's so funny?"

"Nothing." He cleared his throat. "Sorry. That came out wrong. I just love how you three always stick up for each other. You're like a street gang." He gestured toward Brooke's left arm, then Charlotte's, then Georgia's. "That's why you still wear those ratty friendship bracelets, right? It's like your gang tattoo."

Brooke glanced down at the bracelet on her wrist. It was pretty ratty, the plaid pattern long faded. Maybe it *was* time to take the damn thing off. But she wasn't going to be the first to do it. In eighth grade, at a county fair, she, Charlotte, and Georgia had bought matching patterns on a goofy whim, mostly to poke fun at their own obsession with fashion.

"I thought you said we're like a trio of backup singers," Georgia muttered, blushing as she avoided Ethan's gaze.

"He came up with that line when he was in his 'special place.'" Charlotte brought her thumb and forefinger to her lips and puffed on an imaginary joint.

"How many times do I have to tell you?" Ethan protested. "I don't —"

"Smoke pot," Brooke cut in. She removed her sunglasses and lowered her voice. "But you don't *really* think the new girl is all that hot, do you, Brennan?"

"Well, I mean, she —" Ethan bit his full lower lip, his

cheeks flushing slightly. "She actually said something about you, Brooke."

Brooke's eyes narrowed. "Why? She doesn't even know me."

"Yeah, I know, but . . ." A mischievous smile crept across his stubbly face.

"What?" Brooke pressed.

"She thinks *you're* hot," he said. "I mean, not like she's attracted to you or anything. And I know you hate when people say this . . ."

"What?"

"She said you look like Snow White," Ethan finished.

Georgia and Charlotte burst out laughing. Even Brooke had to smile. It was a classic, a perennial — all part of the never-ending, attempted Disneyfication of her life. Every single Silver Oaks member had tried to force the label on Brooke at one time or another. *How pretty you are! You look just like Snow White!* Maybe they figured if they said it enough, Brooke's life *would* become a G-rated fairy tale. Maybe that was what they expected from a girl whose father was president of the board of Silver Oaks.

Perfection.

Yeah, right.

"And when did Valerie have this amazing epiphany?" Brooke asked, flicking her hair over one shoulder.

Ethan shrugged. "She was looking at the photo gallery in the dining room this morning. I think she felt a little lost and out of place, so she just struck up a conversation with me, asking if I knew the people in the photos. You know, the people her age."

"Sort of like how she's striking up a conversation with Marcus now?" Charlotte suggested, her voice dripping with sarcasm. "Because she feels *so* lost and out of place?"

Brooke gazed at Valerie and Marcus from behind the protective shield of her dark lenses. In Brooke's experience, there were only two reasons why a busty, blonde, beautiful girl would compliment the looks of a complete stranger:

A) She was genuinely nice and incredibly open-minded or B) She had a hidden agenda.

Well, that's fine, Brooke thought mischievously. *I'm glad she thinks I look like Snow White. Maybe I can finally play that pure, sweet image to my advantage. Cinderella versus Snow White, huh?*

Too bad I'll be the one kissing the Prince.

Chapter Two

Mixing Things Up

Charlotte was the first to jump in the pool.

Bad move. She immediately resurfaced and splashed around for a minute, her teeth chattering. *CO-O-O-LD!* After a few sputtering gasps, she brushed her soaking red hair from her eyes and launched into her breaststroke, even though she hated that word. She thought about her breasts (or rather, the lack thereof) way too often.

Charlotte von Klaus had been the first to do lots of things. She'd been the first to make out with a boy (Caleb Ramsey, in sixth grade, in a game of Spin the Bottle that had gotten slightly out of hand); the first to sneak into the downstairs sauna at Silver Oaks (on a dare from Brooke); and the first to take a slug of very pricey Pinot Noir straight from the bottle (after her parents' divorce last year. Luckily, with some brute force, Georgia had managed to wrestle the bottle away from Charlotte and toss it in the recycling bin).

And she was the first of her friends to see a therapist. And still the only one.

The way Charlotte saw it, if you were the first to do something, then you carved out some quality alone time — even if you were in the company of your two best friends.

Or, even if you were in the company of a boy. After all, she hadn't been thinking about Caleb Ramsey when she'd made out with him. She'd been thinking about her math homework, and walking Stella McCartney — the von Klaus family's smelly (male) Labrador — and which *South Park* rerun would be on that night.

So as Charlotte plowed through the icy water, kicking her legs and paddling, she didn't think about swimming. She thought about Marcus Craft.

Out of the corner of her eye, she could see him. Due to the overabundance of chlorine, he appeared extra fuzzy and dreamlike. He was still languorously draped over the side of his chair, chatting up the Hot New Girl who had somehow snuck in under the radar. How had none of them heard of her before today? Even Ethan Brennan knew about her. It was absurd.

Breathe, stroke, kick . . . Breathe, stroke, kick . . . Breathe, stroke, kick . . .

Actually, what was more absurd was that Charlotte had to practice swimming.

For reasons never made clear, Old Fairfield Country Day school — otherwise known as the Tombs (Charlotte coined the moniker herself after a freakish school trip to Washington, DC, but that was a very long story) — required that their students pass a swimming test in order to graduate. This was now the summer before senior year, and Charlotte was in big trouble. Brooke and Georgia would have no problem. Brooke had been a pool girl since birth. And there wasn't a single sport Georgia couldn't master.

Give her a bow and arrow; she'd become an archery champ in days. Hence, all of Charlotte's friends would say good-bye to the Tombs and attend college, whereas Charlotte envisioned herself flunking out and spiraling downward in a self-destructive binge of steak sandwiches until she became a grotesque tabloid headline:

1,543-LB WOMAN IS NEW GUINNESS WORLD RECORD HOLDER FOR FATTEST HUMAN. "CAN'T LEAVE BED!!!" SHE SAYS.

Breathe, stroke, kick . . . Breathe, stroke, kick . . . Breathe, stroke, kick . . .

Charlotte reached the shallow end and nearly bumped her head on the stone steps. *Ugh.* She was about as grace-ful as a squid. Was Marcus watching her? She hoped not. On the other hand, if she started to drown, then Marcus would have to dive in and rescue her. But on the third hand (was there a third hand?), that would violate the Second Unspoken Rule of Silver Oaks, which Charlotte had writ-ten herself:

Thou Shalt Not Poach Thy Friend's Love Interest.

Brooke was clearly interested in Marcus. Though that didn't mean that Charlotte couldn't still check him out. Their parents surreptitiously checked out their friends' sig-nificant others all the time, after all. It was the adult thing to do.

"How's the water?" a boy's voice asked.

Charlotte shook out her soaking red hair and turned to see Caleb Ramsey standing poolside, frowning.

Good lord, did that boy need some sun. As always, at this time of year, his lanky body was even whiter than Brooke's, especially in contrast with his oversized, dark blue swim trunks and his mop of black hair. And as always, at this time of year, he somehow still managed to be completely adorable.

"Freezing," Charlotte said. "It's like *March of the Penguins* in here."

"Seriously, C."

"I am being serious. The good part is, much like said penguins, I have lots of blubber to keep me warm." Charlotte leaned against the side of the pool and rested her chin on her dripping arms, smiling up at him. "Unlike you."

"Will you do me a favor?" Caleb asked, returning the smile. "If you ever fish for a compliment again by claiming to be fat, will you give me permission to chop you up and bury you on the golf course?"

Charlotte stood up straight and saluted, deliberately splashing water on Caleb's knees. "Permission granted."

"Hey!" He laughed and scooted away. "Damn. That *is* cold."

"Once you're in, it gets better. I'm gonna do one more lap. My shrink says exercise is good for me." She launched into the water again.

Charlotte hadn't been able to joke around about therapy at first. She hadn't told Brooke and Georgia that she was even *seeing* a shrink until after her second session, post-divorce last year. Not because she was worried they would think she was a loon (they already knew that), but mostly because she wondered if they'd be hurt. After all, who needed a shrink when you've shared everything with your two best friends since the age of diapers?

Surprisingly, Brooke had been the first to speak up. "I think this is exactly what you need to do, sweetie," she'd said, squeezing Charlotte's hand. (This from the girl whose tenth-grade yearbook quote was: *"Life is far too important a thing to talk seriously about."* — Oscar Wilde.) And Charlotte began to realize Brooke was right. The difference between best friends and therapists? Best friends could and should constantly surprise you. Therapists couldn't and shouldn't. Dr. Gilmore was no exception. He'd worn the exact same paisley bow tie to every single session, now going on number fifty-four.

Charlotte reached the shallow end again, allowing her feet to touch the pool floor. She rubbed the water from her hair and eyes. Caleb was staring at Valerie now, though pretending not to. And Brooke was pretending to read *Elle*, and pretending not to watch Valerie and Marcus as well. Georgia was hurrying into the cabana to change, obviously about to meet Ethan on the tennis courts.

Caleb crouched down beside Charlotte, sitting on the edge of the tile and sticking his feet into the water. He eased them down very slowly, up to his knees, and then cringed, as if it were torture.

"You really are a wimp," Charlotte teased.

"Well, not all of us can be lifeguards." His voice dropped to a whisper. "By the way, have you met . . . ?" He didn't bother to finish the question.

16

"Sort of. I said hello to him, anyway. I still have yet to say hi to *her*."

Caleb glanced up at the lifeguard chair, and then returned his gaze to the water. He kicked his feet absently. "She seems pretty cool."

"Really? Have you talked to her?"

"No. This is the first time I've seen her."

"Easy there, Caleb. You're drooling."

"That's because of *you*, Charlotte," he said, rolling his eyes. "You know, I still haven't gotten over that game of Spin the Bottle."

Charlotte laughed in spite of herself. "Funny. I was just thinking about that."

"You were?" He puffed out his skinny chest. "I was that good, huh?"

"Don't flatter yourself, stallion. Actually I was thinking about how when we made out, you were the *last* thing on my mind."

"Thanks," Caleb said flatly. "I appreciate it."

"I didn't mean it like that. I was just thinking . . . I don't know."

"Very articulate," he mused.

"Hey, go easy on me. I got a C-minus in English this year."

"It's not your fault. You had Mr. Lowry. The guy's a sadist."

"No kidding," she grumbled. Charlotte stretched out and kicked her feet to keep warm. "Anyway, enough about the Tombs. It's summer. No school talk."

"Agreed. May the Tombs rest in peace. So what's with Brooke? She seems bummed."

"I think it's because —" Charlotte bit her lip. She was about to say: *This new girl is stealing her thunder,* but that wasn't fair to Brooke. Besides, Brooke may *not* have been bummed, she may have been deeply involved in an article in *Elle,* a brilliant piece about the "25 Most Creative Ways to Wear Swarovski Crystals!"

"Because of what?" Caleb prodded.

"Because Ethan said the three of us are like a street gang," Charlotte replied, mostly because it was the first thing that came to mind.

"You're a lousy liar, Charlotte von Klaus," Caleb said with a laugh.

"He did say that!" she insisted, trying not to smile. "What? You don't believe me? Ask him."

"No, I believe you. And I agree. I'd say you three are exactly like a street gang. Except, you know, that you're socialites from Connecticut who spend all your time at the country club. That's the only difference."

"Is that what you really think of us?" She stopped kicking and stood, rubbing her wet arms. She wasn't sure why, but Caleb's jab had struck a chord inside her.

"Actually, no, I think that's what everyone else here thinks of you," he said, withdrawing his feet from the water. He made air quotes. "'Brooke, Georgia, and Charlotte,'" he proclaimed in a deep voice. "'The Princess, the Jock, and the Clown.'"

18

"Oh, God," Charlotte murmured, aghast. "That's even worse! Who thinks that?"

"Nobody. I'm kidding. If anything, *you're* the princess." He stuck his big toe in the water and splashed her playfully. "Look, I should run. I have to escape before my parents get here. Are you gonna be around later?"

Charlotte nodded. She shivered and stared at the sunlight sparkling off the tiny pool waves.

"Hey, are you all right?" Caleb asked. "I was just messing around."

"I know, I know." She pushed back into the water. "I'm just in a weird mood. I guess we all are. End of school and everything. And in August we're getting officially inducted into Silver Oaks, and all that crap." Silver Oaks policy dictated that when members' kids turned eighteen — as Charlotte, Caleb, Brooke, and Georgia had — they were inducted as official members of the Club, complete with a glam, glitzy ball and freakishly stuffy "ceremony."

"Yeah, well, welcome to my world," Caleb said wryly. "The world of weird moods." He sighed and turned, disappearing into the pool cabana.

Charlotte watched him go. What was she so upset about, anyway? And why should she care what anybody said about her and her friends, or, least of all, care about Caleb Ramsey?

Maybe because she was scared that this summer *was* going to be more of the same old, same old. More hanging out by the pool. More of the same old banter with the

same old pool *boys*: Caleb, and Ethan, and Robby Miller —
a recent Old Fairfield Country Day graduate — arrogant
and in training to be a frat boy this fall. And Robby's fratty
friends, Mike and Johnny and Billy, who were all pretty
much interchangeable, and were also headed off to college
at the end of the summer.

So maybe it was time to mix things up a little. Maybe
somebody just had to make the first move.

Charlotte leaped out of the pool and marched right over
to Marcus and Valerie, dripping water on the flagstones.

"Hi, again!" she said. "You're Valerie, right? Great to
meet you." She extended a wet hand. "I'm Charlotte von
Klaus. C for short. Welcome to Silver Oaks."

Chapter Three

Nice

It was déjà vu. Georgia Palmer could still anticipate Ethan's every move out on the tennis court. After fifteen minutes, she'd already fallen into the same comfortable rhythm: start slowly with a couple of easy volleys, then drag him from side to side with a few lobs until he was frantically dashing across the baseline — then WHAM! Rush the net and slam when he was least expecting it. He hadn't won a single point yet. Just like last summer.

"Are you sure you want to keep playing?" Georgia called.

"Yeah, yeah. Absolutely!" Ethan panted, wiping his sweaty forehead.

Oh, Ethan, Georgia thought. She bounced the ball, trying to appear calm and casual, like it was any old game with any old guy — not the first game she'd played with her ex-boyfriend since he'd dumped her more than nine months ago.

"This is good for me, G," Ethan added, using the hem of his polo shirt to wipe his chin, and revealing a flash of flat, olive tummy. "Go ahead. Serve."

Georgia hesitated. Did she detect a hostile undertone?

She couldn't tell. Ethan wasn't exactly the hostile type. This was the same guy who had grinned (yes, grinned) when he'd dumped her. Then he'd said, "I'm sorry, G, but this isn't my fault. I like you. A lot. But I don't want to lose my job. I love this job."

That was a direct quote.

Thanks, Ethan! Georgia had wanted to shout. (Or scream. Or sob.) *I'm so happy you like me "a lot"! How sweet. And I'm so glad you "love" your job. Thanks for choosing between us.*

Of course, Georgia hadn't said any of it. She'd just nodded. She'd just accepted it, as if a million other country clubs wouldn't swoop Ethan up in a second. She knew this for a fact: Kenwood, just down the road, had been looking for a new tennis pro ever since their last one ran off to Bali with the owner's sixty-year-old wife.

And sure, maybe Kenwood wasn't as nice as Silver Oaks — maybe their courts were clay instead of grass, and maybe you didn't have to adhere to a thousand rules (unspoken or not) to be a member or employee — but it was still a place where you could earn decent money hitting balls with dinosaurs. Ethan Brennan could be a pro at a club within *bicycling* distance, and he could still go out with Georgia Palmer. He'd still be able to have lunch with her every day. It would be romantic. Even better, it would be a big "screw you" to Silver Oaks.

"Are you sure you want to keep playing?" she called to him one more time.

"Hell, yes!" Ethan yelled.

Georgia juggled the ball. Ethan always looked especially cute in the morning, with his light-brown hair a mess. *Asshole.* "Let's be friends," he'd said, and he'd been saying it ever since the breakup. It made her cringe.

"Um, G. You can serve any time you want. I'm waiting."

"Sorry."

She tossed the ball in the air and . . . *THWAP!* Straight down the center: an ace. The ball slammed into the fence behind him. Ethan didn't even bother to try to return it.

"Wow," he said. "Nice one."

"Thanks," she answered.

"You know, I think you're right," he said with an embarrassed smile. "Maybe I should save some energy for my lessons."

"You're playing great," Georgia lied.

"Don't even try it," Ethan said, twirling his racket and approaching the net. "But hey, time out. I want to talk to you about something."

Georgia frowned at him from the baseline. "About what, your game? You're just a little rusty, that's all." She stared down at her yellow Adidas sneakers. She hated herself for being such a dork; she should be ragging on him. She should be telling him that he was predictable, and how that was never a good thing in tennis. It wasn't really a good thing in life, either. But maybe that was more her problem than it was his.

"Come on, G." He beckoned to her. "This has nothing to do with my game. It's kind of private."

"Ethan," she said, suddenly very uncomfortable. She shifted on her feet. Her navy-blue eyes shot back toward the pool. "What are you doing? I don't —"

"Could I be your escort to the Midsummer Ball?" he interrupted.

Georgia gaped at him. She nearly dropped her racket. "*Excuse* me?"

"You know, the Midsummer Ball?" he said. "When you 'officially' become a member of the Silver Oaks Country Club?"

"I know what the Midsummer Ball is, Ethan."

He climbed over the net and sauntered over to her side of the court. "So what do you say? Don't you think it'll be fun?"

"Ethan, I . . ." If this was a joke, it wasn't a very funny one. Worse, as Ethan drew closer, Georgia caught a whiff of that stupid Walgreen's sports deodorant he wore, a pungent mixture of baby powder and aloe — and, for a second, a wave of nostalgia overcame her, and she almost burst into tears. That deodorant was just so *last summer*. As ludicrous as it was, it conjured up a swirl of fleeting images: their many games (his losses), their long walks around the grounds . . . their kisses.

All at once, Georgia was remembering their first kiss from the summer before. It had been late afternoon, all dappled sunlight, and warm wind. They'd been flirting steadily, volleying compliments back and forth over the tennis net, for a month then. That afternoon, after a tough game, they were heading back to the cabana to change. Georgia had never noticed how amazing Ethan's body was. She'd seen him with his shirt off before, but this time she found it hard not to stare. His muscles were defined in all the right places; his skin was tan and smooth. Their bare arms kept brushing together.

Right outside the cabana they bumped into each other. They'd laughed awkwardly, and Ethan had said, "After you," and Georgia had said, "No, after you," and their eyes met, and the next thing she knew, he'd leaned in and kissed her on the lips, ever so gently. *It's not allowed,* Georgia thought weakly. But all notions of rules flew out of Georgia's head as she felt his warm, soft lips move against hers, and she tasted his sweet tongue in her mouth.

Before she knew what she was doing, her arms were wrapping tight around Ethan's waist and she was drawing him even closer, their bodies pressing together. As their kissing deepened, they moved farther into the cabana, and Ethan backed Georgia up against the wall, right next to where the monogrammed pool robes hung. *There's no going back now.* The phrase echoed in Georgia's head as she felt Ethan's lips slide down her neck, and his hands grip her hips. Her skin flushed hot, so hot she thought they might both catch fire. Ethan pulled back to look at her, catching his breath, and his eyes were bright and hopeful. By way of answering his unspoken question, Georgia reached over, took his head in her hands, and kissed him again, relishing the feel of his curls beneath her fingers, his stubble scratching her chin, and yes, the scent of that stupid deo-dorant. . . .

Jesus.

Now, Georgia gripped her racket and fought to com-pose herself. Her skin felt as flushed as it had that long-ago day in the cabana, and she wondered if it was possible to faint from the heat. Where had she learned that the sense of smell was the most powerful trigger for memories? She was pretty sure she once saw an *E! True Hollywood Story* about how an unstable celebrity went on a rampage after smelling her ex-husband's aftershave on a pillow. . . .

"You're not going to accuse me of being stoned, are you?" Ethan teased gently.

"No — I just wasn't expecting that," she finally managed.

"Don't you see?" Ethan said. "It'll be perfect if I take you to the ball, G. It's *the* big summer event at Silver Oaks. Everybody will be there."

"Yeah, like I just said, I *know* what it is. Especially since, as you mentioned, at this particular Midsummer Ball, I'm supposed to be inducted as an official member of this club. So if you *aren't* stoned, let me ask you some-thing." Georgia's normally soft, shy voice picked up a few decibels. Her muscles tensed. She stared hard into Ethan's wide brown eyes. "Don't you think you might be putting your job as tennis pro in jeopardy? If we go on a date where everybody at this place is actually *obligated* to judge me — out in public — as opposed to judging us in secret, don't you think that might be a risky call?"

Ethan blinked at her.

Georgia took a deep breath. *Wow.* She wasn't quite sure where that little tirade had come from. It felt pretty good, though.

"But it's not a date," he murmured.

"What is it, then?"

"We'd be going as *friends*. That's the whole point. You'll prove to your parents and everyone else that you can rise above the dumb Silver Oaks rules. You know, that even though you *accept* the rules, you're better than them." Ethan flashed a big grin, as if he were trying to sell her an SUV with less mileage than the one her parents had given her for her sixteenth birthday. "Get it? We'll go as friends."

Friends. Georgia's eyes smoldered. A dozen possible responses churned through her mind. Among them: *No, I don't get it. . . . That makes no sense. . . . That's the dumbest thing I've ever heard. . . . If we wanted to rise above their rules, we should have never broken up in the first place. . . . You're an ass. . . .* But the one she settled on was: "Well, I will say this, Ethan. You actually managed to surprise me just now. I wouldn't have thought that was possible anymore."

He laughed. "You sound more and more like Brooke every day. So is that a yes?"

"I'll get back to you. I have to weigh my options."

His smile faltered. "Oh, come on. You're not thinking about going with one of those guys who hang out at the pool, are you? The Robby Miller posse?"

"No, I was thinking more along the lines of the new lifeguard," Georgia replied, even though she didn't mean it. "If I'm even gonna go at all, which I probably won't."

"Oh, come on," Ethan pooh-poohed her. "Of course you're gonna go. And you wouldn't ask Marcus. You hate hanging out by the pool. That's what makes you different from Brooke and Charlotte."

Georgia scowled at him. Somehow, he'd made that sound like an insult. Yes, she was different from her friends, but not all *that* different. Or was she?

Before she could respond, the gate swung open behind them.

The new girl, Valerie, stepped out onto the court. She must have tired of Marcus and the pool pretty quickly, because she'd changed out of her skimpy designer bikini into an equally skimpy designer tennis outfit in less than half an hour. The skirt barely cleared her underwear. Her blonde curls swished in a long ponytail that hung down from under her tennis visor.

Georgia tried not to stare.

The problem was, Valerie wasn't just beautiful, she was *sexy*, and she knew it. The telltale sign wasn't her clothing; it was her racket. She carried a Prince Turbo Shark Oversize. The same racket Maria Sharapova used. And *she* must have known that only serious tennis aficionados would appreciate that. Like Ethan, for example . . .

"Hey," Valerie called over with a friendly wave. "I'm not interrupting anything, am I?"

Even her voice is sexy, Georgia thought dismally.

"No, you're not interrupting anything at all," Ethan replied.

Georgia shot him a disapproving glare. He didn't seem to notice.

"Oh, good. It looked like you guys were done." Valerie paused. "I was wondering, could I play with you?"

Ethan smiled. "Well, I should save my energy —"

"Actually, I didn't mean you, Ethan," Valerie interrupted. "I'm sorry, that was rude." She laughed clumsily and pointed her racket at Georgia. "I mean *you.* This will sound embarrassing, but see, I was watching you play, and I was totally blown away. My name's Valerie, by the way. Valerie Packwood. My parents just joined Silver Oaks."

Georgia arched her eyebrow at Ethan. *Take that! Advantage, me.*

"I'm Georgia Palmer," she said, stepping forward. "And thanks, I'd love to play. Ethan's a little winded, anyway." She glanced over her shoulder. "Ethan, you wouldn't mind tightening up the net, would you? It's loose." Georgia felt sick for how she sounded, a caricature of every grown-up snoot at Silver Oaks, treating Ethan like he was "the help" — but she couldn't stop herself. It was Ethan's fault. He was the one who'd put her in such a mean mood to begin with.

"This place is so great," Valerie said, shaking Georgia's hand.

"Is it?" Georgia mumbled.

"Yeah. It's ten times more fun than the club I belonged to in New York."

Georgia snuck a quick peek at Ethan out of the corner of her eye as he furiously turned the winch on the side of the court, stretching the net so tautly that she wondered if it would snap. "I guess it is all right," she replied. "It's just sort of hard to see if you've been coming here your whole life."

"Okay, you guys!" Ethan called. "The court's all ready. Have fun."

He waved at the two of them, glassy-eyed, and disappeared out the gate.

Valerie leaned in close. "The employees aren't half bad, either," she whispered.

Georgia's muscles clenched. But thank goodness, her lips were stuck in the upright-and-locked smile position. It was a familiar sensation: smile while quelling the insecurity; hang on for the emotional plunge. *Mayday! Mayday! Fasten your seat belts!*

"I guess we do get our fair share of cute employees here," she heard herself say.

"I think I'm gonna love it at this place," Valerie went on. "Your friend Charlotte is really cool, too. I met her just now. She's so funny!"

"Yeah. She is."

"She and that girl Brooke seem really tight," Valerie remarked.

Georgia almost replied, *We're all really tight.* But she

stopped herself. From the other side of the fence, she could hear Brooke and Charlotte whispering and giggling by the pool, something about a rumor of how Robby Miller had been doing keg stands in the billiards room that morning. The fact of the matter was: Brooke and Charlotte's obsession with the same old idle chatter not only bored Georgia, it even pissed her off sometimes.

"Uh . . . so what do you say we play?" she asked instead, loudly enough to drown them out.

"Great! Just so you know, I'm not as good as you are." Valerie shook her head. "So, go easy on me, okay?"

"What's the fun of going easy?"

"Touché." Valerie grinned.

"I'm kidding," Georgia added, hearing the coolness in her voice.

Valerie bit her lip, and then blurted, "Is this some kind of test? Because I feel like I'm failing."

Georgia felt a pang of guilt. What was her problem? Valerie had no idea about the history between Ethan and her, or of the history between Georgia and her friends. Valerie was just trying to be polite. Not to mention brave. She was still an outsider — even if she was a budding supermodel with a Prince Turbo Shark Oversize racket. And if somebody like *that* could let down her guard in front of a complete stranger, then so could Georgia.

"My fault," Georgia said. "School is over, so no tests, right?" She smiled weakly. "Lame joke. Forget it. Charlotte's the funny one, in case you haven't already guessed . . . uh, look, it's really cool of you to come out here and introduce yourself and say all those things about my playing. Seriously. I appreciate it."

Valerie tilted her head. "Whoa," she marveled.

"Whoa, what?"

"I was just wondering . . . is everyone here as nice as you?"

Georgia laughed. "Nope. I'm the only one."

"Then I'll be sure to stick close to you."

Chapter Four

A Dog's Mouth Is Cleaner

By the time the dining room opened for lunch at 11:45, Caleb Ramsey had reached the inevitable conclusion: There was no way he would lose his virginity this summer. Not a chance in the world. He was doomed to three and a half months of celibacy. *Again.*

He didn't get it. (Well, he got it on some level: He was pale and scrawny and commented on stuff that was probably best left uncommented on, but so did a lot of other people.) But he wasn't such a bad guy. For instance, he'd never spiked the Midsummer Ball punch with LSD. No, that would be Mr. Farnsworth, back in '75. And true, Mr. Farnsworth had since grown up to be Brooke's stodgy father — but still. In his disco heyday thirty years ago, he'd probably slept with half the Silver Oaks women. Free love, baby! Then he'd married Brooke's mom. Now he ran a hedge fund. Whatever *that* was. Lucky jerk.

Caleb slumped down on a stool at the deserted dining room bar, turning his back on the photos that adorned the wall. He'd seen enough. What was he even hoping to find there? Every single member of Silver Oaks — officially inducted or not-quite-inducted, newborn or deceased, dating all the way back to 1922 — just kept smiling lifelessly at the untouched linen and polished silver, as they always had. And in a matter of minutes, those empty tables would be packed with those very same smiling faces (the living ones, anyway), fresh from the courts or golf course or pool.

The saddest part was that Caleb had studied the pictures with as open a mind as possible. *Who here is a possibility?* He wasn't averse to going the *American Pie* route, either, i.e., hooking up with a woman his mother's age. But most of those women were plastic surgery disasters. They all bore a freakish resemblance to Mick Jagger, with gaunt, lined faces and rubbery lips — *blech*. And the girls his age were out of the question, too. Okay, he *had* lingered on that photo of Brooke by the pool, taken last summer, in her silver bikini. *Hey, why don't I ask Brooke over the next time my folks are out of town?* But that just gave him the creeps. It would be like hooking up with his sister. And Georgia? She was an inch taller than he was. Plus, she was obviously still hung up on Ethan. She would swat Caleb with her racket if he suggested as much.

Which left Charlotte.

In truth, Charlotte was the only real consideration. She'd pulled off the fantastically impossible stunt of growing up with Caleb — *and* making out with him — and still not crossing the lines of incestuous weirdness (Brooke) or Amazonian impossibility (Georgia). She was a special case.

But she would probably just crack jokes the whole time.

The new chick, Valerie what's-her-face, was obviously out of his league. She was out of Brad Pitt's freaking league. But hey, things could be worse. After all, there was a kind of nobility in preserving one's virginity.

Caleb didn't want to be noble, though. He wanted to get laid.

"Hey, you want to hear something funny, kid?" Jimmy the Bartender asked.

Caleb glanced up. He must have been even more despondent than he realized. He hadn't even noticed the grizzled, grinning Jimmy come in from the kitchen.

"Sure, Jimmy," Caleb said. "I'd love to hear something funny."

"A dog's mouth is cleaner than a human's mouth," Jimmy remarked. "Did you know that? It's safer to kiss a dog! Hah!"

Caleb blinked. "Nope. Can't say that I knew that."

"My son the newspaper man told me that. Pretty nuts."

Somehow, even though Jimmy the Bartender was significantly older, wiser, and just plain weirder than ninety-nine percent of the people he served or worked with, he still was called "Jimmy the Bartender" — and that had always bothered Caleb. All the other staff members were known as Mr. This or Ms. That. (Even Mr. Henry, the creepy maintenance guy.) And the unfair part was that Jimmy was one of the few adults at Silver Oaks who was truly worthy of respect.

"So why the long face, kid?" Jimmy asked. He strapped

on his apron and began polishing the bar glasses. "It's the first day of the new season. Summer's here!"

"I know. That's why I have the long face."

"That doesn't make any sense."

"Neither does the stuff you said about the dog," Caleb said.

"You got me there, kid. Hey, listen. I did you a favor."

Caleb frowned. "You did?"

Jimmy sauntered back into the kitchen through the pair of swinging doors. A moment later he reappeared, bearing a heaping plate of food: the Silver Oaks Club Sandwich, neatly cut into quarters, with a side of fries and a little dish of ketchup. It was Caleb's favorite meal — indeed the very meal he'd been about to order. Nothing drowned sorrow and self-pity better than a triple-decker of turkey, bacon, and mayonnaise.

"What's *this* for?" Caleb asked.

"Well, I saw you loitering in here for the past half hour, and I knew what you were gonna order anyway, so I thought I'd beat the lunch rush." Jimmy winked and went back to polishing the glasses. "I didn't make a mistake, did I?"

"Are you kidding?" Caleb shoved a fry into his mouth. "Thanks a lot."

"Don't thank me. You're the best tipper here. Nobody else ever tips. They just sign for everything. You're gonna send my kids to college."

"Aren't your kids, like, thirty years old? Your son's a newspaper man."

"Okay, my grandkids." Jimmy poured a glass of Coke and placed it beside Caleb's plate. "*Bon appétit.*"

A hand clapped down on Caleb's shoulder.

"Just the man I wanted to see," Ethan said, slouching beside him. He was flushed and his tennis whites were nearly soaked through. He nodded to Jimmy. "A glass of water, please, when you have a second? Thanks. I'm totally wiped."

Jimmy shook his head. "Look at you," he joked. "Some tennis pro."

"Seriously, bro," Caleb agreed. "You really should keep in shape over the winter. Self-improvement. That's the ticket."

Ethan glared at him. "Thanks. I appreciate the advice."

Jimmy placed a glass of water in front of Ethan, and then headed back to the kitchen. "Enjoy, ladies!" he called over his shoulder. The doors swung shut behind him.

Ethan laughed.

"I'm going to have that man fired for insubordination," Caleb pronounced, in an uncanny imitation of his own father. "So what's up, Brennan? How's the first day of the new season? You think Georgia and that new chick are ever gonna stop hogging the courts?"

"Why the sudden interest in Georgia?" Ethan asked, frowning.

"You mean, aside from the fact that I've known her since she was born?" Caleb replied dryly. "Don't worry. I'm the one guy here who poses absolutely no threat to you in terms of the opposite sex. Actually, I was more interested in Valerie. Not that I'd have a chance. Want a fry?"

Ethan rolled his eyes. "No, thanks. But do me a favor? Drop the insecure act. It gets annoying after a while."

Caleb grinned. "I was just telling Charlotte the same thing."

"You were?" Ethan scooped up his glass of water, draining most of it in one long gulp and then wiping his mouth with his arm. "Why? Did you ask her to the Midsummer Ball?"

Caleb laughed, surprised. "The Midsummer Ball? I keep forgetting that you've only worked here two summers. Nobody thinks about the ball, you know, until after July Fourth, at least —"

"Oh, God, no," Ethan muttered, his eyes widening. "It's her. Gotta run."

All at once, Ethan was a blur of motion, gobbling up a handful of Caleb's fries, draining his glass of water, and snatching up his tennis racket. Caleb had never seen the guy move so fast, not even out on the courts. Ethan made a swift beeline toward the glass doors that opened onto the pool patio, and was gone.

Caleb turned toward the main dining hall entrance. *Ah* . . . there she was, Mrs. Eliza von Klaus (she'd kept her last name after the divorce) — in all her nipped, tucked, floral-Gucci-sundress glory. And she'd brought Stella, the family's stinky Labrador. No wonder Ethan had bolted.

Why wasn't the "No Pets" policy ever enforced? That dog wasn't just a menace. That dog was *evil*. It was like something out of a Stephen King novel. It drooled, it stank . . . and, well, here it came.

"Well, if it isn't Caleb *Ramsey*!" shrieked Mrs. von Klaus. She sauntered forward and pecked Caleb on the cheek. "How are you, dear? It's been *eons*."

Caleb mustered a pained smile. "Actually, I saw you last weekend."

"Oh, right!" She laughed and clamped a bony, manicured hand over her mouth. "Sorry, dear. I've been a little out of sorts lately."

"It's okay. I think we all have."

"You say the funniest things!" she murmured. She grasped his shoulder. "Listen, sweetie, I'm trying to find my daughter. I want a quick word with her before I change for tennis. I've got a one o'clock lesson with your friend Ethan Brennan."

Caleb glanced toward the patio. "I think Charlotte's out by the —"

"Down, Stella!" Mrs. von Klaus yelled. "Down!"

Caleb turned back toward his plate. Stella's snout was now resting comfortably on Caleb's french fries, the dog's tentacle-like tongue furiously licking at the Silver Oaks Club Sandwich. Mrs. von Klaus yanked Stella away — but not before the beast managed to pluck a strip of bacon and gobble it down.

"I'd better get him out of here," Mrs. von Klaus grunted,

dragging the dog toward the patio doors. Stella's paws scratched the wooden floor. He started whining. Apparently, he felt robbed. Caleb could relate. "I can find Charlotte myself!" she added shrilly. "Don't worry about me, Caleb!"

Caleb opened his mouth. But before he could reply, she slammed the patio doors behind her. He let out a long sigh. "Okay, Mrs. von Klaus," he told the deserted dining room. "I won't worry."

He began to debate how to leave the plate of barely touched food without offending Jimmy (probably best just to bolt, Ethan-style) — when the patio doors burst back open, and in strolled Marcus Craft.

Crap, Caleb thought.

If Caleb clung to any impossible dream of losing his virginity this summer, that dream had just died. This guy was good-looking to the point of being unreal. He shouldn't even *be* here. This was Connecticut. He should be in Hollywood, starring on *The O.C.* It wasn't fair.

Marcus's lifeguard shift was over; he'd wiped the zinc from his nose and changed into his Silver Oaks polo shirt, shorts, and pool sandals — and Caleb could just imagine all the awful, embarrassing comments all the women would make, young or old. . . . Actually, best not to go there. He'd gone there when Ethan had showed up two years ago. And all Caleb had gotten out of *that* was a summer of bitterness and angst, listening to the Silver Oaks women fawn over the "handsome new guy." Even worse, Ethan hadn't turned out to be shallow or stupid or mean, so Caleb couldn't even hate him.

Maybe Marcus would turn out to be cool and funny, too. That would be just perfect. Yep. In that case, Caleb might have to run away and join a traveling circus.

"Hey," Marcus said. "You're Carter, right?"

Caleb laughed in spite of himself. "Caleb," he corrected.

Marcus pulled up a stool and sat beside him, eyeing his plate. "Hey, dude, can I ask you something? Do you go to Old Fairfield Country Day?"

"Uh . . . yeah. Why?"

"Why do you call it the Tombs?" Marcus asked.

"My friend Charlotte made it up." Caleb hesitated. "It's because of a deep, dark secret. The school is built on an ancient Native American burial ground." He lowered his voice and hissed, "There's a curse on it! It's haunted!"

"Oh." Marcus glanced around the empty room, as if he hadn't heard. Either that, or he longed to be somewhere else. Caleb couldn't exactly blame him.

"Nah, I'm just kidding," Caleb said. "It was actually built on a toxic waste dump." He paused. Still no response. "Kidding again! See, Charlotte came up with the name because we went on this field trip to Washington, DC, last year. We got separated from the group, and we wound up at this really strange bar called The Tombs. And they let us in, even though we're underage. And it was

41

filled with a bunch of college kids who looked exactly like everybody you see on those Young Republican websites —"

"Charlotte?" Marcus interrupted, finally paying attention. "The weird redhead?"

Caleb laughed stiffly. "The what?"

"You know. The chick with the flat chest."

Caleb didn't answer. For a second, he wondered what it would feel like to punch Marcus in his upturned nose.

Marcus didn't seem to notice, however. He pointed to Caleb's sandwich. "You gonna eat that?"

"Excuse me?"

"Well, see, employees get a fifty percent discount on meals. But if you aren't hungry, I'll have it. That way I get to eat for free. I'm just asking. You know, if you aren't gonna touch it." Marcus glanced up at him.

Caleb smiled broadly. "Be my guest," he said.

"What's so funny?" Marcus demanded.

"Nothing," Caleb said. "Inside Silver Oaks joke."

"There seem to be a lot of inside jokes around here," Marcus mused.

"I guess there are. It's that kind of place."

"Figures," Marcus said.

And with that, the New Sex God of Silver Oaks shoved the sandwich that Stella had sampled right into his mouth, without even so much as a thank-you. And in spite of Caleb's urge to gag, he began to feel better. Maybe this summer wouldn't be so terrible after all. It might very well turn out to be the best Silver Oaks summer ever. Marcus Craft *wasn't* another Ethan Brennan.

Caleb clapped Marcus on the back and rummaged through his bathing suit pocket, fishing out a soggy twenty-dollar bill, which he promptly slapped down on the mahogany bar. It was Jimmy's tip, very well deserved. And then he marched out the patio doors into the chilly June sunshine.

Chapter Five

Formal Attire

"Marcus is the sweetest guy in the world," Brooke declared dreamily, not caring how corny she sounded. She sighed and glanced up from her untouched dinner. "I finally caught up with him just now. I was about to write off this whole day. I was about to write off this whole *summer*."

Charlotte blinked at her across the candlelit table. "What do you mean, *you caught up with him*?"

Brooke arched her eyebrow and giggled. "What do you think I mean?"

Charlotte giggled, too. Georgia, however, could only manage a faint smile as she cut into her tuna steak. "Makes it sound like you were chasing him. Literally," Georgia murmured.

Well, Brooke thought, shaking the ice in her glass of Diet Coke. *Maybe I have been.*

As soon as Brooke had witnessed New Girl Valerie — she of the big blonde hair and perky, trying-too-hard vibe — shamelessly *throwing* herself at Marcus that morning, Brooke had kicked into high gear. Nobody — *nobody* — snagged a guy before Brooke Farnsworth. But, despite Brooke shooting the sexy lifeguard telepathic *look-at-me* messages all morning and considering actually undoing the strings of her Versace halter bikini, Valerie (in the same bikini) had hogged Marcus's attention. Finally, Brooke, steaming, flung down her *Elle* and stomped off to the cabana to shower, deciding that nighttime would be the best time to make her move. After all, the staff of the country club were all supposed to attend the first formal dinner of the summer, so she knew Marcus would be there, undoubtedly looking delish in "formal attire."

She'd dressed carefully, finally deciding on a black, strapless Prada dress. With her silky raven hair flowing down her back and her red-painted toenails peeking out of her black open-toed mules, Brooke knew she was majorly overdressed, even for the Silver Oaks dining hall (true to form, Charlotte was in a floral-patterned vintage Betsey Johnson sundress, vintage cardigan, and flip-flops, and Georgia in Michael Kors capris, a white tank, and beaded flats).

But Brooke's outfit had paid off, big-time. Seconds before sitting down with her friends, she'd been heading to the bathroom to check on the status of her Dessert lip gloss (flavor: Juicy) when she'd run right into the lifeguard himself. And, as predicted, he looked jaw-droppingly hot in a crisp, blue button-down, silver tie, and khakis, his thick golden hair artfully tousled.

"Hey," he'd murmured, his lips curling up in a grin. "I know you. Weren't you at the pool this morning?"

Ding ding ding! Contestant Number One is going home with the big prize!

"That was me," Brooke replied softly, running her pinkie over her glossy bottom lip. "How was the rest of the day? Save anyone from drowning?" *Make out with any trampy girls named Valerie?*

Marcus shook his head, still grinning. "Didn't get a chance to show off my skills." Then his big blue eyes traveled slowly up Brooke's body and he nodded appreciatively, clearly well aware that Brooke was showing off *her* skills.

"Well, we've got the whole summer," Brooke said, stringing her words together slowly, her eyes focused on Marcus's chiseled face. Understanding seemed to bloom there, because his eyes lit up and he nodded slowly. Then, Brooke — never one to waste an opportunity for playing the flirt — took a step closer to Marcus, breathed in his sweet, clean scent, rested her hands on his shoulders, and kissed him on one warm, slightly rough cheek. "Nice to have you on board," she'd added, her voice barely above a whisper. She could feel Marcus's body respond to her nearness right away.

"See you at the pool tomorrow?" Marcus whispered back, swallowing hard.

"See you, Marcus," Brooke replied, walking backward toward the ladies' room. "It's Brooke, by the way."

"Brooke," Marcus echoed, lifting one hand, his eyes shining.

And Brooke had stepped into the restroom, her heart pounding like crazy, every inch of her knowing that, in some small way, she'd won over Marcus Craft.

"So-o-o?" Charlotte asked at the dinner table, bringing Brooke back to the present. "What *did* happen with Marcus just now?" Charlotte flashed a grin and shoved a forkful of tuna steak into her mouth. "Did you guys, like, do it in the bathroom?"

"Wouldn't you like to know?" Brooke teased. She loved letting her friends think that she was naughtier than she really was. She glanced toward the glass patio doors — now made a mirror by the starry night sky — and caught a glimpse of herself. She did look hot, didn't she? Hotter than the new girl, certainly. She pushed her salad out of the way and leaned forward over the tablecloth. "You don't think that Valerie girl is coming here tonight, do you?" she hissed.

Charlotte shrugged.

Georgia paused in mid-bite, then placed her fork on her plate. "I . . . um, I actually think she was planning on coming," she said quietly.

"How do *you* know that?" Brooke asked, furrowing her brow.

"We, um, we played tennis today," Georgia explained, studying her dinner. "She's actually — well, not so bad."

Brooke laughed. "What, you guys are BFFs now?"

Charlotte laughed, too, only her laughter wasn't as mocking as Brooke's. "Seriously, G. She seemed like a total bitch when I spoke to her at the pool."

Bee-BEEP! Bee-BEEP!

Georgia's cell phone cut Charlotte off, much to Brooke's

chagrin. She didn't want to let Georgia off the hook so easily. Tennis with the *new* girl?

"Sorry, you guys," Georgia said, her cheeks pink. She glanced at the phone under the table, then frowned, then smiled, then picked up and turned from the table. "Hello?"

Charlotte nudged Brooke's knee. "Ethan," she mouthed.

"Who else?" Brooke mouthed back, rolling her eyes.

Georgia held one finger against her ear. "I can't hear you. . . . The reception sucks. . . . What? . . . Really? Okay. Sure. Where? Um . . . no. That's no problem at all. I'll be right there." She clicked the phone shut, shoved it back into her sequined Ya-Ya bag, then sat up straight.

"Everything all right?" Brooke asked.

Georgia shook her head, clearly distracted. "Yeah. I just . . . my dad. I have to meet him. He's waiting for me outside in the driveway. We have to get my mom at the airport. Her flight from Milan came in early."

Brooke shot a quick glance at Charlotte. "Your mom's flight came in early, huh?"

"Yeah," Georgia answered, swallowing her glass of Pom.

"Face it, G," Charlotte stated. "You're a pretty lame liar. Even lamer than me."

"Look, you guys, my dad *is* waiting for me outside." Georgia pushed away from the table and slung her bag over one shoulder. "We have to get my mom at the airport. It's a two-hour drive. She's flying into JFK."

Brooke resisted the temptation to snort. "G, tell your dad to get your mom at the airport by himself. You haven't even finished dinner yet. This is our tradition. We always eat together on the first night —"

"You're the one who said you didn't want any more of the 'same old, same old,'" Georgia interrupted, but in the next instant her face blanched. She knew she'd crossed the line with Brooke.

"Oh?" Brooke snapped, raising her eyebrows.

"Look, I've got to go," Georgia said, standing up and giving an awkward wave. "We'll meet up tomorrow." And then she was gone.

For a long moment, Brooke sat there, puzzling over Georgia's weirdness. Then she decided to, in the words of her idol, Mariah Carey, "shake it off." She had better, bigger things to think about.

Like how and when she was going to hook up with Marcus.

Chapter Six

Meet the Pool Boys

Charlotte tapped her Mademoiselle-pink fingernails on the tablecloth. Twenty minutes had passed since Georgia's mysterious departure, and Brooke was clearly still off in Marcus dreamland. Not that Charlotte was *too* worried about Georgia. Obviously, the poor girl had rushed off to meet Ethan somewhere. Which was unacceptable. He could *not* go on torturing her like this. What worried Charlotte more, though, was how Georgia seemed to be championing the new girl. Georgia was the shy one; it wasn't like her to make new friends quickly — *or* stand up to Brooke.

At the pool that morning, Charlotte had written Valerie off as a typical pampered princess. She'd babbled on about her old school in New York City. (Was it Spence? Or Dalton? And was there a difference?) She'd also talked about how she was sad to leave the city, and how she hoped that Old Fairfield would be a nice change. . . . Blah, blah, blah. Charlotte had tuned her out. The last thing Silver Oaks needed was a girl even more spoiled than, well, Brooke.

But Charlotte had also talked to Marcus. She hadn't told Brooke her take on him. He'd given Charlotte the once-over — the way Charlotte herself might examine an iffy dress at some pricey boutique. Then he'd turned his attention back to Valerie. And that was a big strike against him. Boys shouldn't examine either clothes *or* girls that way. Boys should give girls the Stare.

The Stare was another phrase Charlotte had coined (like the Tombs) and all good boys gave it. Not good as in "well-behaved boys" but good as in attractive, sweet, normal. In spite of its suggestive, stalker-like connotation, the Stare wasn't supposed to give a girl the willies. It was a brief, eye-meeting acknowledgment that you were a member of the opposite sex, worthy of respect — and maybe potential hook-up material down the road.

And Marcus hadn't given it.

Then again, maybe he *didn't* find Charlotte worthy of a hookup. But whatever. It wasn't up to Charlotte to try to dissuade Brooke from going after him. If he *was* an asshole, she'd find that out for herself. Maybe he was just an asshole to redheads.

"You know, I think I'm gonna take a walk," Charlotte said, pushing away from the table. "If I eat the profiteroles, I think my stomach will explode."

Brooke raised her eyebrows. "You aren't going to chase after Georgia, are you?"

"Of course I'm going to chase after Georgia."

"We really need to stop spending so much time

together," Brooke moaned, cupping her chin in her hand. "We're starting to get like one of those old married couples who don't even have to talk. It's creepy."

"Don't go looking for any other strange boys," Charlotte warned Brooke, before standing and heading out the patio doors. Charlotte rubbed her arms through her light cardigan. *Man.* It was chilly tonight. Her eyes roved over the scented torches and the glowing pool water — then she frowned. Robby Miller and his crew were lounging by the pool, playing poker, shirtless and in backward baseball caps. Charlotte wanted to roll her eyes at the preppy fratness of it all.

"Yo, C!" Robby called. "Come here. We wanna ask you sum'm."

For guys who'd spent their entire lives at Connecticut prep schools, Robby, Mike, Johnny, and Billy somehow managed to converse as if they'd grown up in the Bronx. Charlotte wondered when the white homeboy thing was going to go out of style. Hadn't it already?

"Yo, R!" she joked flatly. She strolled across the flagstones, her arms wrapped tightly around herself. "Aren't you boys worried about pneumonia?"

"Stop using big words," Robby snorted, and the other guys guffawed.

Charlotte pasted a big phony smile on her face. "Didn't mean to make you feel stupid," she muttered, glancing toward the ivy-covered fence and listening for any sounds of Ethan and Georgia. She knew the tennis courts had been a favorite nocturnal make-out spot for them last summer. Which, even Charlotte had to admit, was kind of romantic.

"So, what's up with the new girl?" Robby asked, laying his playing cards on his flat stomach. "What's her story?"

Charlotte shrugged. "NYC rich girl. I thought your family knew her."

"Who told you that?" Robby narrowed his beady eyes.

"Ethan did, this morning. He said that her family was friends with your family." Charlotte tapped her foot, bored.

Robby shook his head, puzzled. "I've definitely never met Valerie. And trust me, I would have remembered. She's got it going *on*."

The other three laughed, and high-fived one another. Charlotte briefly considered jumping into the pool again — and staying there. "Hey, have you guys seen Georgia or Ethan?" she demanded over the din. *Stupid pool boys.*

"I'm right here, Charlotte."

She jerked and whirled around. Ethan was sitting off to the side in the shadows at an empty table, still in his tennis whites. She'd walked right past him and hadn't even noticed. *Yikes.* She pulled up a pool chair and flopped down beside him — very deliberately turning her back on the still-raucous pool boys.

"Hey, what's up?" she asked, eyeing him. "I thought you were with Georgia."

Ethan shook his head. Something was wrong — Charlotte could tell even in the dim flicker of the torches and pool lights. His face was drawn. His eyes were distant.

She leaned forward. "Hello? Earth to Ethan?"

"What? Sorry. I'm just a little..." He took a deep breath and forced a smile. "I'll put it this way. I don't think I'll be hanging out with Georgia anytime soon."

"*Really?*" Charlotte wrinkled her nose. "Didn't you call her just now?"

"No." He fixed her with a curious stare. "Why? Did somebody call Georgia and say it was me?"

Charlotte blinked, suddenly confused. "No. She said that her dad called...." Her voice trailed off. Maybe Mr. Palmer really *had* picked Georgia up in the driveway. Maybe they *were* going to meet Mrs. Palmer at the airport. What the hell?

Ethan sighed. "Well, if you're looking for her, you might want to try the golf course. I saw her heading out that way, like, five minutes ago."

"The golf course?" Charlotte asked, flabbergasted. Georgia didn't even play golf. And at nighttime, the course was swarming with crickets and mosquitoes — well, maybe not *swarming*, but it was buggy enough to rule out as a hook-up spot. Besides, who was Georgia even going to hook up with?

"Yeah, she probably figured it was the one place where I wouldn't try to track her down," Ethan mumbled. "She didn't even know I saw her."

Charlotte looked him straight in the eye. "Ethan, what is going on?"

"I — I... well, I asked if I could take her to the Midsummer Ball," he stammered.

"You *what*?" Charlotte asked. She chuckled. She couldn't help herself.

Ethan's soft brown eyes hardened. "What's so funny?" he demanded.

"Um, nothing." Charlotte ran a hand through her red curls. "It's just sweet. And it's sort of an unexpected move, considering the reason why you broke up with her." She paused, a thought dawning on her. "Are you thinking of quitting or something?"

"No!" Ethan answered — too quickly, Charlotte thought.

"I'm gonna go find G," she said, abruptly standing. Ethan was acting weird, Georgia had snuck off to the golf course, Brooke was in love with a jackass ... the world was off-kilter.

For the first time in recent memory, Charlotte felt like the normal one.

Chapter Seven

The Not-So-Secret History of Silver Oaks

Ouch! Georgia swatted her bare arm. That was the third mosquito bite in the last five minutes. She'd forgotten how buggy it was out here.

The last time she'd snuck out to the golf course at night was four summers ago, when Charlotte insisted that she, Brooke, and Georgia conduct a séance to conjure up the ghost of John Lennon. Needless to say, their psychic powers hadn't worked. They'd sat in a circle near the 13th hole, trying not to giggle, with their eyes closed and hands clasped (and Georgia didn't even know for sure who John Lennon *was* at the time) until Mr. Henry, the maintenance guy, stumbled upon them as he was setting gopher traps, causing all three girls to shriek loudly enough to be heard back in the dining room.

"I should have been smart like Charlotte and worn a sweater," Georgia grumbled out loud. She cast a longing glance back toward the cozy lights of the pool and the cabana. Maybe she could just bolt back there and —

"It's nice to know that New Yorkers aren't the only ones who talk to themselves." A laughing voice came from the darkness.

Georgia clasped a hand to her chest. She breathed a sigh, her heart pounding, and then laughed. "Hey, Valerie," she called to the approaching silhouette. "You scared me."

"Sorry to sneak up on you like that," Valerie apologized, rolling her eyes. "I ran back to my car to grab a couple of hoodies. It's cold, you know? Want one?" She extended a velour Juicy hoodie, which had clearly seen better days.

"You read my mind," Georgia said gratefully. "Thanks." She slipped into the warm sleeves.

Valerie fiddled with her blonde curls. "Well, thanks for meeting me. My parents didn't want to do the dinner thing here but I couldn't bear a whole night at home." She glanced around the shadowy expanse of the golf course, spread before them like a giant, rumpled green quilt — and then up at the sky. "Wow. Check out the stars."

Georgia lifted her head. Funny. She hadn't bothered to look in a long, long time. "Yeah. We're pretty near the ocean."

"Cool." Valerie twirled a strand of her hair again, wrapping it around a finger. "Listen, I had a blast playing tennis with you today. I didn't even mind getting whipped. And that's saying a lot. I come from a hyper-competitive family. My brother, Sebastian, takes sadistic pleasure in beating me at any sport."

"Well then, you and I have lots in common," Georgia replied. "Aside from a brother, that is. I love sports."

Valerie nodded. "You *did* seem into the game."

"Yeah, I guess I was just working out some aggression. . . ." Georgia sighed. She was *not* going to think about

Ethan again. Screw him and his stupid Midsummer Ball invitation. She wouldn't think about Brooke and Charlotte, either, because if they knew he had invited her, that would set off an entire *summer* of incessant poolside chatter.

"Ow!" Valerie slapped her neck, jerking Georgia back to reality. "I should have brought some bug spray."

"I'll add that to the Unspoken Rules," Georgia mused. "Thou Shalt Bring Off! to the Golf Course at Night."

Valerie glanced at her, clearly intrigued. Her blue eyes glittered in the moonlight. "The Unspoken Rules?"

"Yeah." Georgia blushed, wondering if Brooke and Charlotte would hate her for giving away their state secrets. Then she decided she didn't care. "At Silver Oaks there are Spoken Rules, and there are Unspoken Rules."

Valerie laughed. "Sounds interesting. Can you give me some examples?"

Georgia's throat tightened. "Well . . ." Okay, maybe she *did* care.

"I'm sorry if this is making you uncomfortable," Valerie cut in. "Hey, I've got an idea. Why don't you tell me about the most scandalous thing that ever happened here? That was always a big pastime at my old tennis club in New York."

"I really should let Charlotte or Brooke tell those stories," Georgia found herself saying. "They're a lot more . . ." She wasn't sure how to finish.

"Gossipy than you are?" Valerie suggested.

Georgia laughed despite herself. "Exactly." Then she paused. "But I can get my gossip on when necessary."

Valerie stepped closer. "All right!" she encouraged. "Now you're talking."

Georgia *was* talking, wasn't she? As she and Valerie hunkered down on the cool grass, the words started pouring out of her mouth "Well, you know that Silver Oaks was founded in 1922, right? The 'Roaring Twenties.' They used to make their own gin in the basement of the Main House during Prohibition. Actually, that's sort of the tradition: You can be as bad as you want, as long as everyone else is, too, in the right ways. You have to have the right pedigree. Charlotte, Brooke, and I are the only fourth-generation members left, so we're supposedly 'special.'" She made air quotes.

"Special?" Valerie repeated.

"Yeah. Our great-grandparents were among the founders. The ones who used to make the gin, in fact. So we're the heirs. Or heiresses or whatever. Caleb Ramsey is third generation, so he's a close second. None of us have any brothers or sisters, either. Maybe that's why we're all so . . . I don't know." Georgia paused. "Close. We call it a 'Family Institution,' right? But it's a majorly dysfunctional family. I mean, everybody keeps each other's secrets about liposuctions and stuff."

"What else?" Valerie asked eagerly, hugging her knees to her chest.

Georgia blushed again. "Well . . . take my own family, for instance." She couldn't believe she was telling this story. "At Charlotte's parents' wedding, which was held here — but they're divorced now — my mom got really drunk at the ceremony. She started shouting, 'I admit it! I'm Jewish!' But nobody cared, because the guy who built this place was named Mort Goldstein. And then my mom passed out on the dance floor in the middle of that cheesy Barbra Streisand song 'Memories'... Which is sort of funny, not only because of the Jewish thing, but also because everybody here always forgets everything, anyway. . .." Georgia broke off, blushing.

Valerie had collapsed, laughing hysterically. "Stop!" she cried. "It's exactly like my old club!"

"Oh." Once again, Georgia was unsure of what to do or say. She fiddled with the zipper of her hoodie. Her eyes wandered back toward the lights. If she was really going to give Valerie the inside scoop on Silver Oaks, then she should probably start *from* the inside, where it was nice and warm and packed with people. On the other hand, it felt pretty good to be on the outside, especially with another outsider.

Valerie sat up and dusted off her True Religion jeans. "That was brilliant." She sighed.

Georgia shook her head. "Just embarrassing —" She stopped, squinting in the direction of the cabana. *Wait a second*. Somebody was walking toward them. . . . Definitely a guy. And for a delirious instant, Georgia's hopes soared. *Ethan.*

"Hey!" The guy waved. "I was hoping to find you out here."

Georgia's body sagged.

It wasn't Ethan. It was the new lifeguard, Marcus.

"I guess I'll see you later," she said to Valerie. She stood up and started to slip out of the borrowed hoodie.

Valerie jumped up, too, and grabbed her arm. "Wait. Where are you going?"

"I just . . ." Georgia glanced between her and Marcus. "You probably . . . I figured you'd probably want to be alone with —"

"I probably *what*?" Valerie interrupted. "Georgia, you just blew off your two best friends at dinner to come out here and talk to me. I'm not going blow *you* off for some guy — no matter how cute he is. I mean it."

Georgia blinked. As always, a dozen different questions spun through her mind before she could manage to speak. But in the end, they all faded as Marcus Craft sidled up beside them, looking frustratingly gorgeous in a blue shirt and khakis.

"So what are you two lovely ladies doing out here, all by your lonesome?" he asked, as nonchalantly as could be.

"Why, waiting for you, of course," Valerie answered, winking at Georgia.

Georgia grinned but all she could think was, *Brooke is going to kill me.*

Chapter Eight

Double Betrayed

Brooke kept sliding deeper into the seat at the empty table. She shouldn't have stashed those Gummy Worms in her Gucci clutch. She hadn't planned on *eating* them. But that was what happened after being ditched at dinner by her two best friends. She glanced at her watch, an old, silver antique keepsake from her dad. Ten fifteen. *Damn.* The plates had been cleared; the last stragglers had finished their dessert ports; even Jimmy had vanished.

The patio doors opened. Her heart swelled. Had Marcus returned, hoping to pick up where they'd left off?

Nope. It was Caleb.

His curly black hair stuck straight up, as if he'd just stepped in from a wind tunnel. He was wearing some sort of ridiculous, fuzzy, homespun-ish brown sweater — something he'd most likely dug out of the trunk of his car, thinking nobody would be around to see it.

"There you are," Caleb mumbled. He sat down in Georgia's long-abandoned seat. "I've been looking all over for you."

Brooke's recently reglossed lips twisted in a puzzled smile. "You have?"

"Yeah." His teeth chattered. "Man, it's cold out there. What ever happened to global warming?" He eyed Brooke's metallic clutch, sitting on the rumpled white tablecloth. "You got any of those Gummy Worms left?"

"Gummy Worms?" Brooke echoed, pretending to be offended. "I didn't bring any candy, Caleb. I came for dinner."

"Oh, give it a rest. You always bring Gummy Worms." Caleb reached for her clutch, fiddled with the buckle clasp, cracked it open, and then frowned. "Lip gloss, wallet, eyeliner —"

"*Excuse* me," Brooke interrupted. She snatched it away from him before he could unearth her you-never-know condom stash. "That's my purse, you jackass. It's private." She sighed. "So what's up, Caleb? Were you hoping I could help you smuggle that sweater out of here without anyone seeing it?"

"Ha, ha," he said, rolling his eyes. But the sound was hollow, even for a fake laugh.

"Are you okay?" she asked, softening her tone. "It's me, Brooke, remember? The candy addict?"

He tried to smile. "Well . . . I feel weird asking this." He lowered his voice. His black mop of hair began to tumble down in his eyes. "This really is private. You know, even more than the contents of your purse." He focused on the tablecloth. "Is everything all right between you, Charlotte, and Georgia?"

Brooke blinked. She felt an odd, unpleasant flutter in her stomach. Maybe that was just the Gummy Worms.

"As far as I know," she answered coolly, tossing her hair. "Why?"

"Well, I was looking for Charlotte just now. And Ethan told me that she'd gone off to look for Georgia. Out at the golf course. And —"

"The golf course?" Brooke cut in. "Why there?"

Caleb shrugged. "That was my question, too. Ethan said that he'd seen her heading off toward the back nine —"

The patio doors burst open with a wobbly *BOOM*.

Charlotte swept into the dining room, looking even more disheveled and distraught than Caleb. Her hair was in what she called "Fire-in-the-hole" mode: an explosion of red curls in every direction, and her cardigan was open, exposing the silky Betsey Johnson. "Come with me, you guys," she stated gravely. She beckoned to Brooke and Caleb, propping one of the doors open.

Brooke exchanged a quick glance with Caleb. He hopped out of his seat. It took her a little longer to hop up; her knees were a little shakier. Plus, she was wearing heels.

A blast of ocean wind struck Brooke's face as she chased the two of them across the pool patio, toward the paved path that led past the tennis courts out onto the golf course. The unpleasant flutter in her stomach upgraded to a full-fledged churning.

"Hey, Charlotte," she called. "What's going on?" Brooke hated being left out of *anything*.

"Shh!" Charlotte hissed. She whirled around and raised a finger to her lips, pausing at the path entrance. "We can't talk anymore after this. Just follow me, and don't make a sound. You'll see. . . ." She tiptoed out onto the path.

Caleb followed obediently, mimicking her every motion, down to the hunched form of her back.

Brooke stood there, unable to move. She watched them scramble onto the golf green, ducking down like burglars. Normally, an insane scenario like this would have sent her into a fit of hysterics. But for some weird reason, she was legitimately worried. Georgia had obviously lied about running off to meet her dad. Duh. But if Ethan had caught Georgia sneaking out to the golf course, it obviously meant Georgia *hadn't* ditched Brooke and Charlotte to meet him. Which meant . . . what?

This was all getting very complicated. Too complicated for summer.

Brooke raced after Caleb and Charlotte onto the golf course, teetering in her Manolo mules. *No need to worry.* In all likelihood, Georgia had used the phone call as an excuse to be by herself. Brooke told little lies all the time, as did Charlotte. If you needed to be alone, you needed to be alone. But any other form of betrayal was, in Brooke's book, not to be taken lightly.

Charlotte and Caleb crept behind the shrubbery near the 2nd hole. Charlotte waved Brooke over, and gestured wildly toward three shadowy figures perched at the edge of a distant sand trap. Caleb's eyes followed. His jaw dropped.

Bunching up the skirt of her Prada dress, Brooke crouched low beside them and squinted, struggling to keep her balance. Gradually, her vision began to adjust to the dim moon and starlight.

Now she understood why Charlotte had looked so shocked.

They'd found Georgia. They'd also found Marcus and Valerie.

"Is this some weird threesome thing?" Caleb asked.

"Shut *up*!" Charlotte hissed.

Brooke's stomach squeezed again. Not just one betrayal. A double. Georgia Palmer had simply decided that the hot new lifeguard and the hot new chick were better company than the two girls she'd grown up with, and who were closer to her than her own family. She'd also conveniently decided to ignore the Second Unspoken Rule: Thou Shalt Not Poach Thy Friend's Love Interest.

Unless she was just helping Valerie do the poaching.

"Should we say something?" Caleb stage-whispered. "Why all the secrecy?"

In the darkness, Charlotte and Brooke exchanged an understanding glance. Both girls knew that they couldn't say anything *now*. They'd deal with it when they saw Georgia tomorrow.

Brooke got to her feet, shaky in her heels on the grass. She knew Charlotte would try to be the big person when confronting Georgia about her lie. But Brooke didn't want to be a big person.

She was one heartbeat away from planning revenge.

Chapter Nine

Hang-Ups

Charlotte decided to make the call at 9:00 a.m. Sunday morning.

Georgia would be up by now. Knowing her, she would have already stretched and worked out to a Pilates video. The entire Palmer family always went a little exercise-crazy over the summer. Charlotte could picture the scene in their Martha Stewart–perfect kitchen: the three of them, all goddamn perky, bustling around in their tennis whites, brewing the first pot of coffee.

Not quite the von Klaus family, was it?

"Honey?" Charlotte's mom called from downstairs.

Crap. Charlotte rolled her eyes. She was in her ratty tank and boxers, flopped back on her four-poster bed among all the ragged stuffed animals she refused to throw out. She clutched her shiny silver cell phone to her chest. "Yeah?" she yelled back.

"Did you walk Stella?"

Charlotte groaned. "Later, Mom. I promise."

Thank God the house was so big. Since the divorce thirteen months ago, it had grown even bigger. Charlotte and her mom could literally go days on end without bumping into each other. As for Dad, he was trouncing around Manhattan with Little Miss Graduate-Degree-in-Business, otherwise known as Rachel Monroe, who because of her "brains" (not because of her size-D cup), had made Dad "feel like a man again." Those were the exact words Dad had used. *To Charlotte.* (Even Dr. Gilmore had been appalled.) But at least he'd had the decency to leave Mom and Charlotte this fine eighteenth-century manor, once featured in *House & Garden*, while he played out his mid-life crisis in an apartment Charlotte refused to visit. Charlotte had already transformed his "study" into a "blast-My-Chemical-Romance-loudly room."

"Okay, then, sweetheart, I'm off to the club," Mom called back. "That darling Ethan is giving me a special tennis lesson! Do you want a ride?"

"No, thanks!" Charlotte yelled, thinking she'd rather walk there barefoot.

A moment later, Charlotte heard the blessed sounds of the garage door opener.

Ah.

A paw scratched at her door, followed by a plaintive whine.

"I would sell my soul to Satan for some quiet," Charlotte said out loud. "Satan? Are you out there? Do you hear me? I'll offer bargain rates!"

She hopped out of bed and stormed over to her door, allowing Stella to shamble in. The dog could never stand to be alone. He jumped right up on the covers, nestling in among the stuffed animals with a contented sigh.

Too bad you're so cute, she thought angrily.

Charlotte tossed her hair over her shoulders, tugged up the strap of her tank, and dialed Georgia's cell.

"C?" Georgia answered on the first ring. She sounded out of breath.

Suddenly, Charlotte felt a twinge of nerves. She sat on the edge of her bed. "G, what's going on?" She jumped right into it.

"What do you mean?"

"Why did you ditch us at dinner last night?" Charlotte asked, chewing on her thumbnail. "Why didn't you just tell us you went to meet Valerie and Marcus?" Charlotte still remembered the shock she'd felt while watching that random trio. She and Caleb hadn't stayed for much longer once Brooke had left, so Charlotte didn't know what the three of them had ended up doing.

There was a brief silence on the other end. "You *followed* me?" Georgia asked, incredulous.

"I thought you were going to see Ethan."

"I was going to meet Valerie," Georgia stated tersely. "Just Valerie. And you guys were being so weird about her that I —"

Charlotte laughed. "Of course we were being weird. We don't *know* her. And isn't it obvious that she's trying to get Marcus?"

There was silence. Then Georgia spoke up. "Maybe she was just being friendly."

"Well," Charlotte replied, fiddling with her friendship bracelet. "He's not such a catch anyway."

Georgia cleared her throat, then gave a nervous laugh. "Hey, how about instead of going to the club today, I pick you up and we go shopping? We can look for outfits for my July Fourth picnic."

"Well, okay. Sure." Charlotte managed a smile. "That sounds like fun. I'll call Brooke —"

"Wait. That's my other line," Georgia cut in. *Click.*

Charlotte's smile faded. Something was going on with Georgia, but she couldn't figure it out. Something in her voice was different — edgy — *click.*

"Hey, C, I gotta run," Georgia said. "I'm sorry. It turns out I can't go shopping today. I really am sorry."

"Stop apologizing," Charlotte said quietly. "It's okay. We'll shop next week." She held her breath, hoping that Georgia would come clean with who was on the other line, and why she'd broken her plans as suddenly as she'd made them.

"Cool," Georgia said.

There was another click, then silence.

Charlotte stood and began pacing her bedroom. She was half-tempted to get extremely pissed off, call right back, and give Georgia a piece of her mind. . . . But then she thought better of it. Maybe she should take the Zen, calm, Dr. Gilmore approach, to give Georgia time to express her side of the situation. Still, why *not* get pissed? Georgia had pretty much hung up on her. In the seventeen years they'd been friends — well, at least since they'd been old enough to talk on the phone — Georgia had only hung up on her one other time, and that was by accident.

Charlotte immediately dialed Brooke.

"Hello?" Mr. Farnsworth answered.

"Oh, hi!" Charlotte hadn't expected *him*. But the snooty Mr. F never intimidated her. "I thought I called Brooke's cell phone. Did I dial your home number by mistake?"

He gave a grunt that, from a more pleasant person, might have been a chuckle. "No, Charlotte. You dialed Brooke's cellular phone. It was sitting on the kitchen counter, so I picked it up." He cupped his hand over the mouthpiece. "Brooke, dear? It's Charlotte. In the future, can you please inform your friends that nine-twenty on a Sunday is a little early to be calling?"

Charlotte groaned inwardly. Brooke's dad took supreme pleasure in acting like a royal tightass.

"What's wrong, C?" Brooke answered, her mouth full.

"Sorry to call so early," Charlotte mumbled.

"Oh, *please*. Don't pull that with *me*."

Charlotte sprawled across the bed beside Stella. "I called Georgia and she was really bizarre."

Brooke laughed. The sound was short and brittle, without any humor. "Shocker."

"Then I think she got another call from Valerie Packwood."

"What makes you think that?"

"I don't know. Maybe Valerie called to gossip about how hot Marcus is —"

She stopped herself. That was a dumb thing to say. She didn't want to add to Brooke's woes. But on the other hand, Brooke didn't even really *know* Marcus. Maybe she *shouldn't* be interested in him. True, he was hotter than anyone who'd ever passed through the Silver Oaks gates since like 1922, but that was no reason to lose all perspective.

"Well, I for one intend to do something about this," Brooke stated.

"You do?"

"Hell, yeah. But don't worry. Nothing too bad. I'm Snow White, remember? I'm pure and innocent."

"Brooke, you're freaking me out," Charlotte said, half-kidding.

"Come on," Brooke groaned. "Listen, what does Valerie what's-her-face have that I don't have? So she's stunningly gorgeous. So she just moved from Manhattan, so she has that mystique and glamour and all that crap. But she does have a strike against her: She's friends with Robby Miller."

It was a punch line. Obviously. Brooke was waiting for Charlotte to laugh. You couldn't mention Robby Miller and *not* laugh. But even as Charlotte tried to muster a chuckle, the sound died in her throat. "You know what's weird, B?" she confessed. "Last night, I asked Robby Miller if he knew Valerie — you know, because Ethan said that her family was friends with his family — and he said that he'd never even met her."

Brooke didn't answer.

"B? Did you hear me?"

"Yeah, C. I heard you. I'm just figuring out how to incorporate that juicy little tidbit into my master plan."

Click.

Before Charlotte could inquire about the exact nature of this master plan, her other best friend had hung up on her, as well.

Charlotte tossed the phone aside. It bounced on the mattress, landing between Stella and a stuffed penguin.

Two hang-ups in one morning: not the cheeriest start to a day.

Brooke wouldn't do anything rash or crazy, would she? She wouldn't do something she'd regret later on, right? No. Of course not.

As Charlotte slid on her flip-flops and ambled out of the room to shower, she remembered those stupid words Dr. Gilmore had told her while wearing that stupid paisley bow tie.

"Lying to yourself is never a solution."

Chapter Ten

No Competition

Georgia nudged her SUV along the Silver Oaks driveway. 9:53. That didn't leave her a whole lot of time. Valerie was due to arrive for their tennis date at ten. Still, Georgia could catch a quick few minutes with Marcus alone by the pool, and explain a couple of things to him.

Namely: They were going to be friends. That was all.

Georgia had deliberately pulled her hair into a sloppy bun and worn her most drab tennis outfit: a sleeveless, white, collared jumper that her mom always sneered at. *"I don't know why you wear it, dear; the design just isn't becoming."* Which was the point. She didn't want to be "becoming" today. Not in Marcus's eyes.

Under any other circumstances, Georgia would have parked her car herself. But if she did that, she knew that she would just sit alone in the lot, and crank a cheesy Top 40 Sunday morning countdown, and lose her nerve. There was a precedent for this: Last summer, after Ethan had dumped her, she'd parked and listened all the way to song #5 — some rap ballad about a "mack dissing his shorty," and it was so dumb and perfectly apropos that she'd ended up weeping.

With a quick punch on the gas, she swerved up in front of the main doors. There was just something so . . . *country club* about valet parking. Brooke and Charlotte never had a problem with it. Of course they didn't. They were comfortable with *being* country club. And why shouldn't they be? Actually, the real question was: Why couldn't *Georgia* be?

For some bizarre reason, Jimmy the Bartender was handling valet duties.

He waddled over to the SUV, dressed in the perennial rumpled Silver Oaks polo-and-shorts uniform, his socks pulled high — then opened the door for her and extended a hand to help her out. She scooped her racket off the passenger seat.

"Hey, Jimmy," she greeted him. "What's going on? Where's the usual guy?"

"He's coming in late," Jimmy answered hoarsely. "Probably hungover."

Georgia shrugged. Hangovers after the first Saturday night of the season were practically expected.

Jimmy climbed in and handed her a ticket stub. "Hey, your friend Snow White is looking for you."

Georgia frowned. "Brooke? She's *here*? She never gets up before ten on Sunday."

"Yeah, she seemed to be in a big hurry to get into the water, too. She drove up in her bathing suit! I told her she would catch cold. But you kids seem to play by your own rules. Hell if I understand." Jimmy closed the door and drove off toward the parking lot, disappearing around the bend.

Georgia absently crumpled the parking ticket in one hand.

Hell if she understood, either. She hurried through the front doors, breaking into a jog in the main hall, past the sitting room and the parlor, and through the empty dining room. Finally she dashed out onto the patio, where she jerked to a stop.

There was Brooke all right, lounging poolside in her striped Shoshanna bikini, but at her side, in a lounger of his own, was Marcus Craft. The lifeguard station was abandoned, but it didn't matter — there was no one in the pool at this early hour. From the way that Brooke and Marcus were positioned, with their loungers so close they were practically touching and Marcus's hand resting ever so casually near Brooke's thigh, they looked as if they might be lying in bed together. Brooke's face was turned to Marcus, and her expression was rapturous. Georgia's stomach gave a jump; maybe it was Brooke she needed to talk to, even more than Marcus.

She padded over to them, her flip-flops thwacking, and took a deep breath. It was Marcus who looked up first, shielding his eyes from the sun and flashing her a grin.

"Georgia on my mind," he crooned, his voice sing-songy. Instantly, Brooke's head snapped around, her hazel eyes like ice.

Georgia felt her throat catch. She wished her cheeks weren't turning pink quite so rapidly. Last night had been *crazy*. Soon after Marcus had joined them on the golf course, it had been obvious that he was into Valerie — he kept touching her curly hair and teasing her about her ratty hoodie. But after the three of them had chatted for a while — just bullshitting — Georgia grew paranoid, thinking that she heard whispers coming from the shrubbery just beyond where they sat. Valerie announced that she was beat and needed to get back home. She kissed a disappointed-looking Marcus on one cheek, asked Georgia to meet her for tennis at ten, and flitted out into the night like some blonde, Juicy-clad pixie.

Georgia and Marcus remained alone, regarding each other in the bright starlight. Georgia could no longer hear any noises in the shrubbery, or much of anything. Her chest hurt every time she took a breath, and she found herself noticing the sharpness of Marcus's cheekbones, the way his upper lip curled slightly. She wanted to say something to him about Brooke, something about the fact that her friend said that he was sweet, but then Marcus was taking a step closer to her.

"I noticed you at the pool this morning," he murmured. "I couldn't take my eyes off you."

"Really?" Georgia asked, her voice high-pitched. She hadn't remembered Marcus even glancing her way. But then she wanted to kick herself. Why did she always sound so stupid around boys?

"There are so many beautiful girls at this club," Marcus had gone on, his voice still low. "But there's something . . . different about you."

Georgia had wondered if Marcus would be saying the exact same thing to Valerie had *Georgia* been the one to flit off into the night.

"I guess I *feel* different," Georgia found herself saying, in the nervous, rambly way she sometimes spoke around boys. "I mean, not like I feel like I don't fit in, but Brooke and Charlotte — those are my best friends — they're so a *part* of things here, and I'm just this sporty girl who . . ."

"You're not *just* anything," Marcus protested, his hand now coming to rest on Georgia's arm. And then, before Georgia could say anything, or stop him, he was inclining his head toward her, and coming in so close, and his lips were almost on hers.

As she felt his mouth approach, her immediate thought was of Ethan, the last boy she had kissed. Sadness welled up in her, and then she thought of Brooke. Her best friend. Hadn't *she* kissed Marcus tonight? Brooke had implied as much at dinner.

This was all wrong.

"Marcus," Georgia gasped, giving his chest a shove and taking a step back. "No — I can't — we need — we can be friends, but we can't be anything more. . . ."

The corners of Marcus's mouth turned down, and he'd begun to protest, but Georgia, by then full-time freaking out, asked if they could just talk tomorrow at the club. Her head was spinning and she knew she needed to go home and try to sort through everything. To make sense of it all.

And now here she was, confronting Marcus and Brooke, unsure of how to begin. She tried not to stare at

Marcus's body. His stomach looked as if it had been carved from Sheetrock.

"What's up?" Marcus asked, still grinning.

"N-not much," Georgia stammered. "I'm going to play tennis with Valerie." She began to tug on her racket strings. She wished Brooke would stop staring at her with such naked hostility. What did she *know*?

"Hey, G, I wanted to ask you something," Brooke suddenly said, her voice stony.

"Mmm-hmm?" Georgia could feel her face getting hotter.

"Do you know if Valerie knows Robby Miller's family?"

Georgia glanced up from the strings. *That* certainly hadn't been the question she'd been expecting. "Yeah . . . didn't Ethan say that she knew the Millers?"

Brooke trailed a hand through her black hair, stretching her petite, flawless body across the cushions. "That's what I *heard*," she replied slowly. "But Charlotte said that Robby Miller told her he never met Valerie. Don't you find that sort of weird?"

"I, uh . . . I don't know," Georgia said. She shook her head, growing increasingly flustered. "What are you getting at?"

"The point is, Valerie must have been lying," Marcus replied.

Georgia glared at him.

What the hell? Where had *that* come from? He sounded pretty sure of himself for somebody who'd only known

79

Valerie for, like, a day. And pretty sure for somebody who seemed happy not only to *scam* on Valerie, but on Georgia, as well . . . and now Brooke. Besides, who *cared* what Robby Miller said? When had *he* become a pillar of honesty? The most likely scenario: Robby had tried to get in Valerie's pants once during some summer in New York, and had been rejected, so now he wanted to protect his reputation with the Pool Boys.

"Hey, your tennis partner is here," Brooke stated in a cold, dry voice. She nodded toward the patio doors.

Georgia turned. She never imagined she'd be so relieved to see a girl who was hotter than she was, more stylishly dressed, *and* carrying a superior racket to her own. But then, she'd never imagined a lot of things that had happened in the past twenty-four hours.

"Well, I guess I'll catch you guys later," she mumbled, hurrying away. She beckoned Valerie toward the tennis court path.

"Hey, are you all right?" Valerie asked, peering at Georgia from under her visor. "You're all flushed."

"It's nothing." She hurried across the pavement. "Just psyched to play a good solid set."

"Um, okay."

Georgia turned the corner — and froze.

Ethan was out on the far court with Charlotte's mom.

Georgia knew that over the summer, he conducted a few special lessons on Sunday mornings for "beginners." She watched, holding her breath, as Ethan volleyed the ball as politely as he could, smiling encouragingly the whole time, the way one might play with an eager but not-so-coordinated toddler. He'd shaved, too, his tennis whites were pressed, and his brown eyes were sparkling. Mrs. von Klaus, decked out in a tight tennis outfit, was practically drooling over her racket, and Georgia could see why.

In that moment, Georgia wondered how she could have ever let herself be attracted to Marcus. Really, when looking at Ethan, she felt like there was no competition. And all at once, for no reason whatsoever, her eyes began to burn.

"Hey, Georgia?" Valerie asked.

Georgia opened her mouth, but the words caught.

"You know, we don't have to play tennis," Valerie went on. "I'm happy to go for a swim or leave you alone, or whatever."

"I . . ." Georgia drew in a brief, shaky breath. "No." She wiped her eyes and managed a strained laugh. "You're right. I'm sorry. I just don't really want to play tennis right now."

"Sorry for what?" Valerie arched an eyebrow. "Honestly, I didn't feel like getting my ass kicked again, anyway. If I'm gonna forge some kind of rep at Silver Oaks, I can't be *losing* all the time, can I?"

Georgia laughed again.

"Oh, you find that funny, do you?"

"No. Well, yeah. It's just — thanks for letting me freak out for a second." Georgia wondered if Brooke or Charlotte would have been as supportive.

Valerie shook her head. "If that's what freaking out means around here, then I'm in big trouble," she said.

"Where I come from people have breakdowns and melt-downs and every other kind of 'downs' you can imagine all the time. Your freakout *so* isn't on that level." She paused by the green. "Hey, I have an idea."

"What's that?" Georgia asked shakily.

"How do you feel about golf?"

Georgia stared ahead at the course through her misty eyes. Just last night, they'd been there. With Marcus.

"I gotta tell you, I'm really bad at golf," she finally muttered.

"So am I." Valerie patted her shoulder. "All the more reason to play. It'll be much more fun, right? No competition."

Chapter Eleven

Crashing Kenwood

So this is what my life has come to.

On Sunday morning, Caleb gazed up at Eliza von Klaus from a leather armchair in the Silver Oaks parlor, and wondered — for a horrifying, pitiful, surreal moment — what it would be like to hook up with her.

Not that he would ever act on it. Not that he could even attempt to try. But the thought did flit through his mind. And hey, was it really so wrong? Right now she looked pretty good, post-tennis lesson, when she wasn't all made up, fresh from the court in her white nylons, her red hair in disarray.

I made out with this woman's daughter. I am going to hell.

"So what finds you here, dear?" Mrs. von Klaus asked. She eased down into the armchair across from him, sipping a bottle of Fiji water. "You know, somebody should really redecorate this room." She wrinkled her nose at the mahogany bookshelves. "It's so *drab* in here."

"Well, I think it was the smoking room once," Caleb suggested.

Mrs. von Klaus threw her head back and cackled, as if he'd told an outlandishly hysterical joke. "You are a laugh *riot*, sweetheart," she proclaimed in a shrill voice. "So, tell me. Do you play tennis at all?"

Caleb shook his head, and shifted in the seat. The leather squeaked under his khaki carpenter shorts. Maybe he should leave. Yes. He was here to hide, anyway. Earlier, he'd strolled out toward the cabana, in a carefree mood — nothing on his mind except another day by the pool — and then he'd spotted Brooke and Marcus on some loungers by the shallow end. They looked pretty much as if they'd made a pact to go ahead and do the nasty right there. So he beat a hasty retreat to the dining room, but not before he caught a glimpse of Valerie Packwood chatting up Georgia out on the path by the tennis courts. What the hell was going on with that new friendship? And so he made a beeline for the one place where he couldn't *possibly* run into members of the opposite sex — this dusty old room lined with books nobody read, and arranged with furniture nobody ever used.

At which point, Mrs. von Klaus showed up.

"Well, my divorce lawyer told me that playing tennis is a great way to meet single, older men," she was saying. "What do you think?"

Caleb blinked. "Huh?"

"Do you think tennis will improve my love life?" She wriggled her eyebrows.

The leather chair was beginning to feel like quicksand.

"I think your lawyer's in a better position to answer that than I am, Mrs. von Klaus," Caleb croaked. "Well, it was nice talking to you, but I should probably be —"

"Nonsense!" She threw her head back and cackled again, then hopped up and patted his knee. "You stay right here. I'm sorry to have barged in on you like this. I'll see you soon, sweetheart!"

Caleb watched her go. *Yes. Yes, you will. And that terrifies me.*

Just as Charlotte's mom was trotting out, Ethan came in, his hair messy from playing. He nodded politely at Mrs. von Klaus, then spotted Caleb sitting alone in the middle of the room. He stopped and grinned, puzzled.

"What are you doing *here*?" he asked.

"Trying to hide and failing," Caleb mumbled. He gestured toward the armchair across from him. "Have a seat. It's lots of fun."

Ethan shrugged and plopped down across from him. He dabbed his face with the towel he was holding, glancing around at the meticulously arranged coffee tables and Oriental carpets. "I need a break myself. You know, in two years, I don't think I've ever actually *been* in the parlor."

Caleb smirked. "You look beat, man. Mrs. von Klaus really gave you a run for your money, huh?"

Ethan glared at him. "Have *you* ever tried playing tennis with a beginner?"

"I've barely even tried playing at all," Caleb admitted. "Not exactly the most athletic type, in case you haven't noticed. That's why I like hanging out by the pool. Zero impact. Low stress. Plus, I play poker. I won eighty-nine bucks on Thursday."

"Yeah, well, maybe I should take up poker, too," Ethan said. "God knows I could use the money. . . ." He laughed awkwardly. "Or maybe I could be a lifeguard. Look at Marcus. They stuck him with the morning shift, but he's still got one of the sweetest gigs at Silver Oaks."

"You really think so?" Caleb asked.

Ethan met his gaze, and then looked away. "I'm just sort of sick of tennis."

All at once an idea popped into Caleb's brain. Maybe it was the way Ethan had said the words "sick of tennis"— as if he were trying to hide the fact that he was actually sick of something else, namely Silver Oaks itself. Caleb understood; he was already a little sick of this place himself, and it was only the start of the summer. "Hey, what are you doing right now?" Caleb asked. "I mean, when's your next lesson or whatever?"

"Not until one," Ethan said. "Why?"

Caleb pushed himself to his feet. "Why don't we go check out Kenwood? You know, crash the place? Picture it! We'll just march right in there like we've always belonged. It'll be awesome. Like a movie, right? We're the two zany new guys who just show up unannounced, and scope out the scene . . ." His voice dwindled to silence.

Ethan stared back as if Caleb had just suggested that they hold somebody up at gunpoint. "Have you ever *been* to Kenwood?" It almost sounded like an accusation.

Caleb swallowed. "Uh . . . well, yeah, once. When I was seven. Robby Miller had his eighth birthday party there. You know, the Millers were members at Kenwood before they became members here." He flopped back down.

Ethan took a deep breath. He scooted forward in the chair and perched on the edge of the cushion. "Can I ask you something, man?" he whispered. He shot a quick glance toward the hall, making sure they were alone.

"Yeah. Of course."

"Are we friends? You know — like you and me?"

Caleb started to smile, and then quickly stopped himself. Ethan's face was deadly serious. He wasn't kidding around. Caleb didn't quite know how to deal with the question. Guys didn't ask questions like that. At least, not the guys Caleb had grown up with. They asked questions like: "Where'd you get that pansy-ass sweater, Ramsey?" (Robby Miller had asked him that exact question just last night, which was why it sprang to mind.) "Are we friends?" was a question a girl would ask. Guys didn't probe each other's innermost feelings. They conversed only to exchange vital information: point spreads, profane jokes, violent threats, et cetera.

"What I mean is," Ethan continued, "do you think of me as somebody who works for you, or somebody you actually like hanging out with?"

Now Caleb felt offended. "Wait. You think the only reason I hang out with you is because you *work* here?" He'd *never* been one of "those" rich boys.

"No. It's just . . ." Ethan inched forward a little farther.

"I want to tell you why I don't want to go to Kenwood. And I could make up some BS or whatever, but there's something I want to get off my chest. And I figured you of all people would understand."

Caleb nodded. His pulse picked up a notch. "Sure. Go ahead."

"I applied for a job there." Ethan stared straight at Caleb, his face devoid of expression. "They turned me down."

"Whoa." Caleb leaned back, floored. "Are you *serious*? Why?"

Ethan chuckled sadly. "Maybe because they already have a better tennis pro."

"No, that wasn't what I meant. Why did you apply for a job there? You —"

"Because I can't be with Georgia if I work *here*," Ethan interrupted in a hushed voice. "I didn't *get* the job, Caleb. And I need a job. That's why I'll be giving Eliza von Klaus tennis lessons until the day I die." His eyes darted furtively toward the hall once more. "Listen, just make sure Georgia comes to the Midsummer Ball, okay? It was stupid of me to ask her. . . . I just — I don't know. I couldn't stand the thought of her going with someone else. And I know that nobody at Silver Oaks cares about the ball, and whatever." He bit his lip. "Just make sure she comes, all right? Please?"

"How am I supposed to make sure she comes? You should talk to Brooke or Charlotte. Seriously, Ethan, I'd help you out, but —"

"*You* ask her to the ball," Ethan cut in.

Caleb raised his eyebrows. "Excuse me?"

"You heard me," Ethan whispered.

"I thought you said that you couldn't stand the idea of her going with someone else," Caleb replied, baffled.

"That's why it has to be *you*," Ethan insisted.

Hmm. That sounded like a put-down. But Caleb knew it wasn't. At least he hoped not. "Dude, you're not making any sense."

"If *you* ask her, then she'll know it's innocent," Ethan explained. "She knows you don't like her like that, Caleb. I know you don't like her like that. Everybody knows."

Caleb suddenly realized he was perched on the edge of his own armchair. Did Ethan mean that Charlotte knew? Caleb's heart kicked. "Don't you think it'll be weird, though?"

Ethan shook his head. "Just do me this favor, all right?"

"But what if she says no?" Caleb asked.

"She won't," Ethan stated. He brushed his tousled hair out of his eyes. "She'll just be glad to have an excuse not to go with me. I know it."

Caleb bit his lip. "I don't know, man."

"You're not going with anyone else, are you?"

"Well, no. . . . It's just that . . ." Caleb drummed his fingers on the rumpled legs of his shorts. "I mean, no. But — okay, yes. Well, yes, depending." He spun in the leather chair and peeked over the seatback into the hallway, just to make extra certain he and Ethan were alone. Then he turned back to Ethan, feeling his face grow warm.

"But the truth is, if I was going to ask anyone, I would ask Charlotte."

"You would?" He grinned. "You guys aren't, like, friends with benefits, are you?"

"NO!" Blood pounded to Caleb's face. He knew he must have been bright red. He kneaded the armrest. "I . . . mean, no."

"So what's the problem, then?"

"Nothing."

"Caleb, it's gotta be something. You're losing your shit for *some* reason, bro."

Oh, Jesus. Caleb sighed and leaned back again. How had he even gotten himself into this little interrogation?

"What could be that big a deal?" Ethan prodded. "So, you're not sleeping with Charlotte? Fine. You *want* to sleep with her? Fine. You've never slept with her. . . ." He stopped.

Caleb shut his eyes and prayed that Ethan wouldn't guess.

"Let me guess," Ethan finally said.

"What?" Caleb's eyes opened. He frowned.

"You're a virgin."

"Jesus!" Caleb hissed, whipping around in horror to check the hall, straining his ears for the sounds of footsteps. "Lower your voice!"

But Ethan kept right on grinning. "Wow-ee. You'd better do something about that before you're cast in the sequel to *The Forty-Year-Old* —"

"Ethan, shut the hell up." Caleb wasn't having it.

Ethan sighed, crossing his arms over his chest. "Listen, Caleb, I'm just playing. Who the hell *cares* if you're a virgin?"

Caleb's nostrils flared. "Spoken like someone who doesn't fall on the same side of the virginity fence as I do."

"I'm serious." Ethan laughed, sounding to Caleb much older than his years. "Anyway, I still don't get it. What does losing your virginity have to do with inviting Georgia to the Midsummer Ball?"

"I . . ." Caleb didn't have a response. The Midsummer Ball wasn't like a prom. It wasn't like a debutante ball, either. It wasn't even really *anything* — other than an excuse for every grown-up at Silver Oaks to get drunk again as they toasted their seventeen-year-old children (who also got — not-so-secretly — drunk).

"Because you *really* want to go with Charlotte," Ethan pronounced.

"Yeah, I guess I do," Caleb admitted. "See, a couple of years ago, we all went on this field trip to Washington. You know, when Charlotte came up with the nickname for Old Fairfield? The Tombs?" He hesitated. He'd never talked about this before with anyone, not even Charlotte herself. "Ethan, you have to swear you won't tell —"

"I won't. God, you're so paranoid."

"Okay." Caleb's voice dropped to a barely audible whisper. "See, Charlotte and I fooled around that night. We got separated from the group, and we were all alone, in this bar, The Tombs, and I got drunk and brave and I kissed her. I honestly thought we would go back to the hotel . . . but then Mr. Lowry caught us. The good part was that he was all freaked out for losing us, so he said that he wouldn't tell anyone what we were doing — if we swore to stay with the group from then on. Charlotte and I never talked about it again . . . but I don't know. It sounds really lame, but I've just always felt that Charlotte would be — the one. And that it would be this summer. And the night of the ball . . ."

Ethan sighed. "It's cool, bro," he said encouragingly. "You're into Charlotte. Maybe she's into you, too. Either way, we'll get you laid this summer. But here's the thing. I bet you taking Georgia to the Midsummer Ball could even be your ticket. I bet because if anything, she'll —"

"Hey, Caleb?" a sweet, melodic female voice interrupted.

Caleb winced, gripping the armrests. He spun around.

Valerie was standing in the parlor archway, her racket over her shoulder and her blonde ringlets spilling down her back. He had no idea how long she'd been there, or how much she'd heard. For all he knew, she'd heard the whole thing.

"Yeah?" Caleb croaked.

"Do you know where I can find some golf clubs?" she asked, her smile giving away nothing at all.

Chapter Twelve

Secrets within Secrets

Tiptoeing down the stairs to the sauna with Marcus Craft filled Brooke with delicious pleasure — and a little nostalgia.

She'd snuck two other boys down here in the past. The first had been Johnny. Yes, as much as it pained her to admit it, in ninth grade she'd made out with Johnny of the Robby Miller Posse — i.e.: the wannabe gangsta with the SNOOP chain. To Brooke's credit, though, Johnny actually had been shy and cute before he discovered the world of hip-hop and poker, and he'd been an amazing kisser. The second had been Clesthenes Demetriou, the son of a Greek diplomat. Tall, olive-skinned, and mysterious: the boy who'd proved to Brooke that there could be "the one who got away." (Or he would have proved it, had he been able to speak English.) He'd said maybe fourteen words total during the entire summer — but when he smiled, she couldn't help but pounce on him. They'd spent morning after morning sneaking off together until his family vanished in late August. After days of inconsolable sorrow, Brooke had received the following e-mail:

brook: ur kisses in sauna made summer very plesent. i back in athens. i wish to maintain letters. i missing u. i also kissed girl named haley burns in sauna. thought u to know. apologies.

SINCERITY,
CLESTHENES DEMETRIOU

All right, so in the long run, maybe it was okay that he got away. Not to mention the fact that Haley Burns was a dyed-platinum blonde with faux boobs. But thankfully, she'd vanished, too, off to LA or something. The lesson learned: Brooke would not allow herself to be that vulnerable again.

"Hey, Brooke?" Marcus asked.

She paused at the bottom step and turned, her pool robe falling seductively off one shoulder. "Yeah?"

"No one's gonna find us here, will they?" he whispered, stepping down toward her. There was a slight wrinkle of concern between his perfect golden brows. "Mr. Farnsworth came to the staff meeting this morning and really drilled into our heads that there was to be no 'fraternizing' between the staff and —"

Mr. Farnsworth. Could there be anything more mood-killing than hearing the boy you were about to make out with mention your *dad*? Brooke rolled her eyes and put a hand against Marcus's soft, warm lips. "It's fine," she assured him. "Trust me?"

"I trust you," Marcus said, raising one eyebrow, his mouth curling up in a teasing smile. Brooke could hear the excitement in his voice. Ever since that morning, when she'd convinced him to get off his lifeguard throne and join her by the pool, she'd known that they'd be alone together by that afternoon. Brooke's only regret was that Valerie wouldn't be around to witness her triumph.

And it kept nagging away at her that Georgia had intruded on their little interlude. But Brooke was *so* not dealing with that girl right now.

With a small smile, Brooke whipped around and headed down the narrow hallway, already imagining that she could feel the hot steam from up ahead. God, she loved sneaking to the sauna. On the brick wall above the sauna door, in three-year-old ruby-red Chanel nail polish, her eyes drifted to the familiar, tiny graffiti scrawled there:

WHAT HAPPENS AT SILVER OAKS STAYS AT SILVER OAKS —
WHERE ELSE WOULD IT GO?

One rainy afternoon, Brooke had written those words, as Charlotte and Georgia laughed and egged her on. They'd been fourteen back then, and boys were in the picture, but not as much as now. Things had seemed so much simpler then, Brooke thought with a sigh.

Marcus chuckled at the words, not knowing that Brooke herself was the author.

"Is that true?" he murmured as Brooke rapped on the heavy wooden door.

"Of course," Brooke replied, listening for a response. Silence. *Perfect.* She turned the knob and she and Marcus slipped into the room, the steam hitting them like a wall. Brooke took a deep breath. The heat was intense, almost too intense, but also sublime. The moisture made her skin feel all glowy and sent tingles of delight down her arms.

Or maybe that was Marcus, walking up behind her.

"The thing is," Marcus was saying, his hand brushing the nape of Brooke's neck. "I just started working here, so I really don't want to screw up."

Brooke spun toward him, her pool robe slipping off almost entirely. "Marcus, if anybody finds us, *I'll* get blamed for dragging you down here. People at Silver Oaks don't fire employees like you."

Marcus stepped closer, grinning, one hand tugging on the bottom of the thin, blue T-shirt he'd thrown on over his swim trunks. "How can you be so sure?"

"Because Ethan Brennan hooked up with Georgia last summer," Brooke replied mindlessly, tossing her hair over one shoulder. "And he's not even half as —" She broke off.

"Ethan hooked up with Georgia?" Marcus asked.

Brooke swallowed. *Oops.* "Yeah. I thought you knew." *After all, isn't Georgia your new best buddy?*

Marcus shook his head slowly. "No . . . I had no idea." His expression was unreadable.

"Let's not talk about Georgia, okay?" Brooke whispered. She slowly lowered herself down onto the tiny two-person bench, the hot rocks sizzling and crackling below. "Let's not talk about anything."

Marcus didn't need any more persuading. He eased himself down beside Brooke on the bench, moved in very close, and wrapped one arm around her. They gazed at each other for one brief, hot moment, and then Marcus leaned in and ran his lips along Brooke's long, pale neck, moving up toward her earlobe. Brooke let out a sigh of pleasure, arching her back, and then she lowered her face and let her lips meet Marcus's. The kiss was long and deep and fierce, and they kept going, Brooke wrapping her arms around Marcus, welcoming the feel of his lean, muscled body against hers. As Marcus's deft hands pushed off Brooke's pool robe, she helped him get his T-shirt over his head. His skin was slick with steam. Marcus broke the kiss and drew back for a second, his breath ragged.

"You know," Marcus whispered, his blue eyes full of longing, "there are so many beautiful girls in this club. But you're . . . you're different, Brooke."

"I know," Brooke whispered back, shivering with joy at Marcus's words. Brooke *had* always felt different from Georgia and Charlotte, as if she were worlds beyond them.

And then Marcus leaned in once more and their mouths locked in another passionate kiss. Brooke drew Marcus back with her along the bench, her nails digging into his bare back, murmuring words into his ear, as he kissed her and kissed her as if he'd never stop. The steam and the heat and Marcus's fingers on her skin were enough to make Brooke dizzy with desire.

This was exactly how she wanted to spend the rest of the summer.

Chapter Thirteen

"Robe"

Charlotte was on a mission. After being hung up on by her two best friends, and dutifully walking Stella, she'd driven straight to Silver Oaks that afternoon in the hopes of finding said best friends. And, secretly, she hoped she might run into Caleb. Though he often got on Charlotte's nerves, she had to admit that the boy had a way of making things make sense when the world got too crazy.

It was Caleb's voice Charlotte heard just as she was stalking by the parlor. *What is he doing in* there? she wondered, pausing and peeking into the room. A strange sight met her eyes: There was Ethan Brennan lounging in a chair, looking laid-back and gorgeous as ever. And Caleb was standing up, facing, of all people, New Girl Valerie. Charlotte felt her jaw drop in shock. Was Valerie . . . *flirting* with Caleb? All the signs were there: big sparkly smile, the occasional giggle. And Caleb's ears were turning redder by the second as he responded to whatever Valerie was asking with soft, shy murmurs. Charlotte's stomach did a backflip. Was it . . . *jealousy* she was feeling? And, if so, why? What did she care about who Caleb Ramsey attempted to flirt with?

But this Valerie person was definitely getting out of hand.

Now *determined* to locate Brooke and Georgia, Charlotte whirled around and flip-flopped out to the pool patio. The water shone glossy-blue and empty. Marcus Craft had abandoned his lifeguard perch and Mr. Weatherby — another balding Silver Oaks mainstay, like Jimmy the Bartender — was in his place, looking none-too-appealing in *his* swim trunks and whistle. Worst of all, Robby Miller, Frat King of the Pool Boys, was sprawled across a lounger, deep asleep in his Señor Frog's T-shirt and board shorts, the brim of his cap pulled low over his eyes. For one horrifying instant, Charlotte felt like she was in a scene from some apocalyptic sci-fi movie: *The Last Girl and Boy Alive . . . and the Boy Is Robby!* Even his usual entourage of pool boys was absent. Charlotte figured they'd probably swaggered into the dining room to stuff their faces with club sandwiches and practice their straight-outta-Compton talk. *Yo, yo, we a crew up in here, can we get some service?*

Rolling her eyes, Charlotte kicked off her flip-flops and marched over to Robby. If he *was* the last boy alive, he might as well make himself useful.

"Hey, Robby? *Psst*. Wake up." She tapped his baseball cap — hard.

Robby Miller squinted up at Charlotte from his lounger and let out a yawn. "I'm sleeping, woman," he grunted.

"I got that," she snapped. "I was wondering if you've seen Brooke or Georgia."

"I'm sure they're around here somewhere," Robby said, jerking his hat farther down over his eyes.

Charlotte scowled. "Thanks."

"I'm not gonna be able to sleep anymore with you hovering over me like this," Robby muttered. "It's like Homeland Security up in this piece." He finally sat up and rubbed his eyes. "You hungry? Come on. I'll buy you lunch."

Charlotte was stunned. "You will? Why?"

"Why ask why, girl?" He grimaced and stood, stretching. "You don't think I got the paper to buy you lunch? Plus, there's something I gotta tell you. I got some dirt on Valerie."

Now he had her attention. Charlotte's green eyes widened. "What kind of dirt?"

"Let me buy you lunch and then I'll tell you."

"Okay, okay — you're on." Charlotte turned and strode toward the patio doors. Inside the dining hall, her eyes roved over the sea of white: the linens, tennis shorts and shirts, and the terry-cloth pool robes. She wondered where Caleb and Valerie had gone off to.

"Don't you want to put on some flip-flops?" Robby asked, trailing after her.

Charlotte stared down at her bare feet and purple-painted toenails. "Why?"

"It's just that Brooke's dad is in there. The Pres."

"And what? I'm supposed to be scared?"

Sure enough, there was Mr. Farnsworth sitting by himself smack in the middle of the room, staring back at her disapprovingly. Charlotte waved. Mr. Farnsworth flashed a brief, perfunctory smile.

"What's he gonna do, Robby, kick me out?" she murmured. "I'll tell you what, let's sit at the bar."

She hurried over to an empty stool, relieved to have an excuse not to sit at a table for two. Frankly, with Robby Miller, that seemed just a little *too* intimate. The moment she sat down and turned her back on the room, however, she felt a tap on her shoulder.

"Charlotte?" Mr. Farnsworth asked.

"Yes?" she said, avoiding his eyes. She stared at the rows and rows of bottles behind the bar. *Hmm.* A bottle of pricey Pinot might be a nice little treat right now. . . .

"You know you're supposed to wear appropriate footgear," Mr. Farnsworth was saying.

"Yeah, I know. But see, Stella accidentally peed on my flip-flops, so I'm soaking them in the cabana sink."

Robby winced.

Mr. Farnsworth remained silent for a few seconds. "I trust you'll start adhering to the rules, young lady," he said. "Enjoy your lunches." He swiftly headed toward the exit.

"Wow, girl," Robby breathed, laughing. "I gotta hand it to you. Nobody else has the *cajones* to talk to him like that."

Charlotte snorted. "Please. He's just looking for an excuse to be holier-than-thou. He's been a jerk ever since my folks split up. He assumed that my dad would stay in Connecticut. Dad's the 'Silver Oaks scion.' And —"

"So, what's up, kids?" Jimmy the Bartender interrupted, a little too cheerily. "I finally got off valet duty, so here I am." He drew two glasses of water and placed them on cocktail napkins, then fixed his rheumy eyes on Charlotte. "Hey, sweetheart, can I have a word with you?" he whispered. He shambled down to the far end of the bar, beckoning to her with a gnarled finger.

Oh, brother. What now? Charlotte followed him, trying not to roll her eyes.

He leaned toward her across the shiny mahogany surface. "You might not want to mention your dog to Mr. Farnsworth," he whispered.

"Why?"

"I just wanted to give you a heads-up. Some of the members have been complaining that Stella's been around a lot. I figured it would be better if I told you before someone went to your mother, what with the rules and all." He patted her hand.

"Jimmy, thank you," Charlotte said. "Seriously. I appreciate it." She set her jaw and moved back along the bar to rejoin Robby.

Jimmy ducked under the bar, and produced two sets of silverware wrapped in white linen napkins. "So what'll it be?" he asked. "Wait! Lemme guess. For you, Mr. Miller, the bacon-cheddar burger, medium, with fries, and for you Ms. von Klaus, the Cobb salad." He vanished through the swinging doors into the kitchen.

Charlotte sighed.

"Hey, C, don't sweat these fools," Robby said quietly. "They dis Stella because they love the drama." He took a sip of water. "It's never about the dog. But if you give them drama, they'll just give you drama back."

Charlotte turned to Robby. That was a pretty smart thing to say. Not to mention semi-sweet. The Silver Oaks Guardians of Moral Values weren't complaining about Stella. They were complaining about Eliza von Klaus. *She* had stayed in Connecticut, whereas Dad had moved away. And everyone liked Dad better. Never mind that he was a cheating slime-ball; he was suave and charming. Mom was kooky and irritating. Robby was dead-on: It had nothing to do with Stella; it was about the fall from grace.

"So I'm thinking of going as Rob from now on," Robby announced, apropos of nothing.

"Sorry?"

"Rob. You know, instead of Robby. What do you think? Rob's a little more adult sounding." He scratched his buzz cut. "I'm starting college in the fall and whatnot. I can't go around anymore sounding like a little kid."

Charlotte wasn't sure what to make of this bizarre pronouncement. Probably best just to ignore it altogether. "Uh . . . so what's the scoop about Valerie?" she asked.

"Here's the dilly." He leaned in close, eyeing the rest of the dining room to make sure nobody was listening. "My dad works for First National Bank, right? He represented the Packwoods on some huge deal. He and Mr. Packwood became pretty tight during the whole thing. The Packwoods ended up moving out here."

Charlotte waited for him to finish. He took another sip of water and cast a longing glance toward the kitchen.

"I'm hungry, yo," he said.

"That's it?" she pressed. "That's Mr. Packwood. What about *Valerie*?"

Robby lifted his shoulders. "Oh. Nothing. I guess that's just why she said her family knew mine."

Charlotte was beginning to suspect that the only reason he'd offered to pay for lunch was because he didn't want to eat alone — or maybe because he wanted to bounce his new "Rob" identity off a female.

"That's the *dirt*?" she finally demanded.

"The dirt is that her dad told my dad that Valerie is all messed up, because all her old friends dissed her. She's a failure. She pretty much flunked out of her old school. She went to one of those crazy private schools in Manhattan, like Dalton or Spence, but they didn't ask her back. That's part of the reason why the Packwoods moved out here. Girl's got issues. Her brother, Sebastian, is going to some Ivy League college next year, so he's all taken care of. Have you seen Sebastian? Boy's got mad gear, yo! Boy rolled up in a Lexus with a platinum-plated vanity license . . ."

Charlotte tuned him out. That wasn't exactly dirt — at least not in the fabulous, sexy, or scandalous way she'd been hoping.

"So that's really it?" she asked. "That's —"

"Lunch is served!" Jimmy the Bartender barreled

through the door, carrying their lunches. "One bacon-cheddar with fries, and one Cobb salad."

Robby scratched his chin as Jimmy set down the plates. "Yo, Jimmy, isn't it pronounced *Cobe*?" he asked.

Jimmy shot a quick glance at Charlotte. She laughed. "*Cobe*?" they both repeated at the same time.

"Yeah. That's how my mom says it." He gestured to Charlotte's plate. "That salad with the bacon and everything. She calls it a *Cobe* salad."

Charlotte chewed her lip. She couldn't stop herself from laughing. She wasn't sure why, but that struck her as the silliest thing she'd ever heard. *Cobe?*

Jimmy waved his hands. "Kid, call it whatever you want." He winked at Charlotte and headed back to the kitchen.

"So what do you think?" Robby asked, chewing.

"About the salad?" she asked.

"No. About the other thing."

"I don't know." She shook her head, staring down at her salad. In spite of how good it looked — Cobb or *Cobe* — she didn't have much of an appetite anymore. "I guess it doesn't matter that she's screwed-up and super-rich, right? Lots of us are."

He frowned at her as if she'd just spoken in Cantonese. "Huh?"

"Valerie."

He whistled dismissively. "I wasn't talking about *her*. I was talking about me. You know, my new handle. *Rob*. Instead of Robby? What do you think?" He gripped his burger with one hand and flashed a peace sign with the other.

Charlotte giggled again. The boy was truly a wonder. She'd always written him off, but what a mistake! How anyone could be so dense and self-involved, yet so honest and genuinely well-intentioned . . . ? If anyone was worthy of the Stare, Robby Miller was. So she gave it to him. A girl giving a boy the Stare! It was empowering!

He didn't notice, though. Of course he didn't. She almost felt like leaning over and kissing him.

"How about *Robe*?" she suggested.

He blinked at her. "Huh?"

She patted his arm and lifted her fork. "Never mind."

Chapter Fourteen

The Bet

Golf was not a sport. Not a real one, anyway. It was a *game*. Which was probably why Valerie was so good at it.

Not to disparage Tiger Woods, but Georgia now knew why every country club boasted a golf course as opposed to, say, a football field. Golf didn't involve exercise (aside from lugging around bags of clubs). It wasn't like tennis, either: A person didn't socialize during tennis. A person faced off against an opponent. Golf was all about *hanging out* with your opponent. It was about laughing and gossiping about cute boys (Valerie's specialty; she even thought *Caleb* was cute). It involved strategy, sure; Georgia could appreciate that. (Or she would have, if she could actually play.)

"Oh, my God," Valerie gasped, dumping her golf bag onto the pool patio. "I am so beat! Are you hungry?"

"I don't think I've ever been hungrier." Georgia sighed.

"What do you say we hose down and change, then grab some lunch? I'll treat. I've been daydreaming about club sandwiches for the past hour."

Georgia nodded distractedly. "Uh . . . sure. You don't have to treat, though." Her eyes drifted over to the cabana, and then toward the pool, in a vague, fleeting hope of spotting Charlotte and Brooke. Maybe the four of them could *all* have lunch together. But instead, she saw only Caleb — strolling toward them in the most absurd pair of sunglasses she'd ever seen: huge, bug-eyed Jackie-O ones that were definitely *not* designed for guys. Somehow, though, with his mop of dark hair and baggy bathing suit . . . he pulled it off. He *was* cute, she had to admit, in a sort of emo-rock-star-like way, like Connor Oberst, the Bright Eyes guy. Not that she would ever tell him that, of course.

"Hey, Caleb," Valerie said, grinning at him slyly as he approached. "Cool shades. Where'd you score those?"

He shifted nervously on his bare feet. "Um . . . Charlotte's mom." He pointed his thumb over his shoulder.

Georgia peered behind Caleb and caught a glimpse of Eliza von Klaus and Theresa Farnsworth lounging together by the diving board in their sarongs and sunhats. Both waved at the same time, looking uncannily like their daughters — which, for some reason, gave Georgia an uneasy feeling. Where *were* their daughters?

"I don't get it," Georgia said.

"Neither do I, really. Mrs. von Klaus offered to lend me these, and it wasn't like I could say no, because it was a pretty nice thing to do, and I, uh —"

"Caleb?" Georgia interrupted.

"Yeah?"

"You're rambling."

Valerie laughed.

Caleb grinned crookedly, blushing. He turned toward

Valerie, and then stared at the patio flagstones. "Sorry. Anyway, Georgia, do you have a second?"

"Sure. What's up?"

Without another word, Caleb ducked behind the wall of shrubbery that marked the entrance to the path leading to the tennis courts and golf course. Clearly, he was making a feeble attempt to hide from the prying eyes and ears of everybody lounging around the pool. He waved her closer.

Georgia exchanged a puzzled glance with Valerie.

"Come here," Caleb whispered.

Valerie raised her eyebrows. She forced a chuckle, smoothing the folds of her white tennis skirt. "Do you guys want to be alone?"

"No," Georgia said, a little too emphatically. Maybe it was the golf or the gossip or her hunger — but she just wasn't in the mood for Caleb's odd brand of humor right now. She took Valerie's arm and dragged her over to Caleb's sad excuse for a hiding place. "There's nothing Caleb can tell me that you can't hear as well."

Caleb hung his head, biting his lower lip. "Okay. Fine. Whatever. This is gonna sound really weird, all right? But, G, I want to ... I want to ... know if you'd go to the Midsummer Ball with me," he said all in one breath — so fast that Georgia wasn't certain if she'd heard him.

She narrowed her eyes, her heart rate increasing. Georgia Palmer had never had so much boy drama in her life. "Huh?"

"I know, I know," he added apologetically. "It sounds

crazy. I mean, because nobody really brings dates, anyway, and it's just this dumb induction ceremony —"

"You're asking me to be your date to the Midsummer Ball," she interrupted.

He tried to keep smiling. "Uh . . . yeah. That's pretty much it."

Georgia's sloppy bun suddenly felt very tight. She yanked out the band, allowing her blonde hair to tumble down over her shoulders. In her tennis shoes, and with Caleb barefoot, she had a good three inches on him. "Why are you doing this, Caleb? What's really going on? Is this a practical joke?" The words spilled out before she could stop them.

"It's no joke," Caleb muttered miserably. "I swear."

All at once, just as fast as she'd gotten angry, a lump formed in her throat. How could she be so stupid? *He's doing this to make Charlotte jealous. He's afraid to admit his feelings for her, the feelings he's always had.* A sad smile broke on her face. If only Ethan could take a cue from Caleb. Yes, insanely enough, she found herself wishing that Ethan would pull what Caleb was trying to pull right now — asking Charlotte or Brooke or even Valerie to the Midsummer Ball. Because *that* would prove that Ethan still had feelings for Georgia. *That* would mean that he cared enough to try to make her jealous.

Caleb pushed his shades back up his nose. "Hey, listen, G. I'm sorry. Forget I brought it up, all right? It's no big deal."

"Hey, Caleb?" she said softly. "I would go to the ball with you; I mean it. But somebody else already asked me."

"Ethan?" Caleb asked, sounding increasingly miserable.

"Yes," she whispered. "Ethan."

"So are you gonna go with him?" Caleb yanked the glasses off, no longer even pretending he wanted to continue this conversation. "Wouldn't he have to quit first?"

"He would, yeah. But he said we'd go as friends. And I said I'd think about it. Honestly, though, I don't want to go with anybody. I mean, it's not really a date type of scenario, you know? And I'm flattered you asked me —"

"I'll go with you, Caleb," Valerie interrupted. "I mean . . . if you're looking for a date."

Georgia stiffened. *Whoa.* She sure as hell hadn't seen *that* one coming. Her eyes darted between the two of them: Valerie, in her tight tennis whites, with her perfect blonde curls (even after eighteen holes of golf), and Caleb, in his soggy bathing suit and borrowed shades clutched in his hand. Valerie *had* said Caleb was cute . . . but was she *really* that into him?

"I . . . uh, well — sure. That would be cool." Caleb began backing away from them and he quickly shoved the glasses back on. "Thanks, Valerie. We'll talk later, okay?" His face was so red it was almost scarlet. He turned and scurried toward the far side of the pool, where the Robby Miller posse was lounging.

"So what was that all about?" Georgia cried, utterly

bewildered. "Do you like Caleb? I thought you liked Marcus."

Valerie drew close to Georgia. "Listen, there's something I need to tell you," she whispered. "I asked Caleb to the ball to protect *you*."

Georgia shook her head. She almost smiled. "You *what*? I don't get it."

"I overheard Caleb and Ethan talking before we played golf. And they said . . . well, they said something, and I'm not even sure what to make of it. But it sounded like they'd made a bet. They were talking about the ball."

"Whoa, slow down," Georgia said. "What are you saying? What kind of bet?"

"I don't know if you want to hear this." Valerie brushed her long blonde curls out of her face. "Ethan made a bet with Caleb. Caleb told Ethan that he . . ."

"That he *what*?"

"That he wants to lose his . . . virginity." Valerie lowered her voice. "So Ethan made a bet with him. He told him to invite you . . ." Once again, she left the sentence hanging.

Georgia licked her dry lips. She felt the color drain from her face. "That can't be right," she whispered.

"I'm sorry, Georgia. I'm just telling you what I heard."

"Okay." Georgia was trembling. "Let me just get this straight. You're telling me that you heard Ethan Brennan make a bet with Caleb Ramsey that if he invited me to the Midsummer Ball, he would lose his virginity to me?" It took every ounce of self-control Georgia possessed not to scream. She could feel the muscles in her throat tighten.

Valerie's deep blue eyes mellowed. "I just —"

"Don't say another word," Georgia snapped, even though she wasn't angry with Valerie. How could she be? Valerie didn't know Ethan or Caleb. She'd just been caught up in a preposterous farce — all the more preposterous because she knew that Valerie was telling the truth. Why not? It was all quite plain: Caleb *had* agreed to this idiotic bet with Ethan. But of course Caleb had agreed; he was a sex-starved boy. What Valerie didn't know, however, was that Ethan had lost his virginity to Georgia. And she had lost hers to him.

Georgia remembered every detail, every sensation. It happened just two weeks before he broke up with her, when everything still felt perfect. In fact, at that time, she'd been so delirious with joy that she hadn't even bothered to hide their relationship from most of Silver Oaks (Brooke and Charlotte, naturally, had known all along).

One Friday night, Ethan's parents were out of town, so he invited Charlotte over to his house — a cozy cabin by Lake Deerwood, three towns over. Although they'd never actually discussed doing it, as soon as Georgia walked in the door and seen the candles on the table, she'd known that *this* night would be the night. Ethan had even cooked for her. (Well, he'd tried; he'd burnt some lasagna, which they washed down with a bottle of his parents' white wine, cracking up the whole time.) Then, they moved to the sofa, where they started kissing, but kissing in a way that they had never kissed before — fierce, passionate, urgent kisses that Georgia knew were going to lead somewhere.

And soon Ethan *was* leading her somewhere, taking her hand and walking her upstairs to his bedroom, where she'd never been before (their increasingly intimate make-out sessions had been confined to the cabana and the golf course at night). They lay across Ethan's bed, still kissing, and caressing. Ethan whispered to her that he didn't care if they waited, and he wanted to do whatever she was comfortable with, but by then Georgia was out of her mind with love and longing, and she was undoing the belt buckle on Ethan's jeans, and whispering that she wanted him, here, now, always.

And it had been slow and awkward and fumbling at first, but Ethan had been so tender and careful and sweet that when it was over, Georgia lay in his arms, flushed and overwhelmed with understanding.

So that's why they call it making love, she realized, turning to smile up at Ethan's radiant face. Because, in those incredible and strange and wonderful moments, she and Ethan had been expressing what could only be called love. They'd never actually said *I love you* to each other, but, as far as Georgia was concerned, this was better. She'd never been so fulfilled.

Now she felt sick.

Because it was all so clear: Looking back, especially in light of this new information, Ethan must have known all along he was going to dump her. Maybe somebody at Silver

Oaks had even warned him he'd get fired if he kept up with her. He'd just wanted to get his jollies and keep his job at the same time. So he'd invited her over. Now he was sloughing off his ex onto Caleb, his "buddy." After all, *he'd* gotten lucky with Georgia. Why shouldn't Caleb?

Georgia heard Ethan's voice in her head. *Hey, man, why don't you invite Georgia to the ball? She's an easy lay. . . .*

"Georgia?" Valerie asked.

"Yeah?" Georgia realized that her hands were balled into fists. She was on the verge of exploding.

"Don't you want to get something to eat?"

"Huh? Oh, no. No." Suddenly, Georgia wasn't hungry anymore. She needed to be alone.

Chapter Fifteen

Bizarro Universe

A few days later, Brooke was still basking in the glow that was Marcus Craft.

They hadn't gone all the way that afternoon, but they'd done enough to get them both too hot and bothered to remain in the sauna. They'd parted ways in the corridor outside, exchanging long, deep, intoxicating kisses, and then, cell phone numbers.

Brooke hadn't heard from Marcus for the past several days — she'd been away from the club, visiting her grandmother in Darien, Connecticut, so she hadn't been in touch with Charlotte or Georgia either. She was still pissed at Georgia for this new Valerie obsession, but Brooke was feeling too satisfied about Marcus to hold a grudge.

On Wednesday morning, Brooke was padding up to the pool patio, grinning. She couldn't *wait* to see Marcus. She hadn't told Charlotte or Georgia about him, but she couldn't wait to do that, either.

This might be the start of something huge, she said to herself as she neared the pool. *This could even be the summer when I finally stop flinging and get into a relationship.*

She laughed out loud. Yikes. Was she already starting to think in lame romantic clichés?

"There you are!" Charlotte cried. She jogged up to Brooke, looking out of breath. "You'll never guess what Georgia just told me —"

Brooke glanced at the lifeguard chair. Mr. Weatherby, Marcus's fill-in, sat there, perusing *Reader's Digest.* Brooke's heart sank.

"I tried calling you," Charlotte was saying.

"I didn't get cell service in Darien." Brooke tucked her hair behind her ear. "Hey, what's wrong? You —"

"What's wrong?" Charlotte cut in. She frowned and fiddled with her friendship bracelet. "How about, what's *right*? Which is pretty much nothing at this point. Georgia has been spending *every* day with Valerie. And I finally saw her last night —"

"How is she?" Brooke muttered.

"Fine," Charlotte answered hastily. "But the point is, she told me that Valerie asked Caleb to the Midsummer Ball."

Brooke gasped. "C, what are you talking about?"

"You heard me. And the worst part is, Georgia just let him say yes."

For the first time, Brooke noticed how upset Charlotte looked — her cheeks were red and mottled.

"She told me," Charlotte went on, her voice cracking, "that it seemed like Valerie had a thing for Caleb and then she just *asked* him. . . . But you know what the most screwed-up part is?"

Brooke shook her head.

"Caleb asked Georgia to the ball first!" Charlotte hissed, her eyes bulging. "Can you believe that? She turned Caleb down because Ethan asked her, but still . . . it's like — it's like — what was Caleb *thinking*?"

"Um, C?" Brooke asked tentatively.

"Yeah?"

"I don't get any of this."

"Neither do I!" Charlotte practically shouted.

"So what you're saying is . . ." Brooke chewed a fingernail. "What *are* you saying? Who invites anybody to the Midsummer Ball, anyway?"

"My sentiments exactly," Charlotte muttered.

Brooke tried to think, to sort it all out — but she couldn't. The only part that she understood was the obvious: Charlotte was pissed that Caleb had asked Georgia to the ball, and even more pissed that he'd accepted an invitation from Evil Valerie. It was so obvious — to Brooke anyway — that Charlotte had feelings for Caleb. It had taken Valerie's presence to get Charlotte to even recognize those feelings.

But the Georgia issue was the most disturbing. Why wouldn't Georgia intercede? Why hadn't she tried to put the kibosh on Valerie? Why hadn't she explained that the Midsummer Ball was a joke (it was in August for Christ's sake, not even a real midsummer night) and that the fun of it was that there *were* no dates, so anybody could hook up with anybody?

"Why is Georgia spending all this time with Valerie?"

Brooke whispered. "It's messing everything up. Didn't you tell Georgia that Valerie is a two-faced liar? We know that she doesn't know Robby Miller's family —"

Charlotte shook her head. "Actually, that's a lie. She *does*."

Brooke scowled. "She does?"

"Yeah. Robby told me. And she's like super-rich, but has all these . . ." She didn't finish.

"All these *what*?"

"Listen, you want to get out of here?" Charlotte suddenly asked. "Let's take a ride, okay? My mom let me have the BMW."

Brooke took a deep breath and forced herself to relax. She'd find Marcus some other time. "Sure," she said. Sometimes, if the universe has been flipped on its head, it was best not to argue. Sometimes it was best to let circumstances take the lead. It was best to surrender control.

Chapter Sixteen

Spying

"Hey, C? I know you were psyched for a drive and all, but you *do* realize we're way out in the boondocks, yeah?"

Charlotte's hands tightened on the wheel as Brooke dug her cell phone out of her bag. She had to give Brooke credit; she'd been *very* patient so far, considering that they'd driven around aimlessly for the past two hours (or aimlessly as far as Brooke knew) — and especially since the radio play had ranged from grim to excruciating. What ever happened to fun, frothy pop? It was all alt-rock: whiny post-pubescent boys lamenting existential crises. Every song followed the same pattern: First the plaintive melody over acoustic guitars (i.e., the sensitive part) followed by the cymbals and thundering chorus (i.e., the angry part). Who *wrote* this crap?

To add insult to injury, the only CD Charlotte's mom had left in the car was a sinister collection of heavy metal covers, sung by a cheeseball named Pat Boone.

"We're almost there," Charlotte said, pulling down the visor to keep from going blind. She glanced at the clock. *Man.* It was nearly six. The sun was sinking fast toward the horizon at the end of the road. "It's right up this little terrace. . . ."

"Why the sudden fascination with the Old Fairfield *über*-mansions?" Brooke asked. She jammed her phone back in her purse. "Come on, C. What's up?"

Charlotte spun the wheel and bounced down a barely paved road toward a white house with a brick chimney, and a pointy shingled roof —

There!

"Look," Charlotte hissed.

She jammed on the brakes. She and Brooke jerked forward in their seat belts.

"C, tell me what the hell is going on," Brooke snapped.

Charlotte tapped her finger against the windshield as she pulled into the shade of a sycamore tree and cut the engine. "Look. See that little white house over there? That's the carriage house of the Whitney estate, which is like the most expensive home in the county. And that's Georgia's SUV in the freaking driveway. And look!"

"Oh . . . my . . . God!" Brooke whispered, her face turning even paler.

The two of them watched, slack-jawed, as Georgia and Valerie strolled down the front walk together, their blonde hair and tennis whites sun-dappled in the spotty shade, followed by Marcus — freshly showered, his hair wet and combed, dressed in a crisp long-sleeve T-shirt and jeans — and then by Caleb, wearing a ratty sweater over board shorts with flip-flops. The four of them piled into Georgia's

SUV, laughing. Charlotte felt as if she were watching some surreal movie with the sound off.

"Interesting," Brooke said in a toneless voice, as if they hadn't just seen their best friend and the new girl with the two boys who were rightfully *theirs*.

Charlotte turned toward her. "Are you pissed?"

Brooke shrugged. She didn't say a word. Instead, she just watched as Georgia's SUV pulled out of the driveway and disappeared around the corner.

"Brooke —"

"Why did we come here, C?" Brooke interrupted.

"Well, ever since Robby told me the truth about Valerie, I've been dying to see where she comes from, so to speak."

"What did Robby say?" Brooke grinned.

Charlotte started up the engine again. There was a lot that Robby had said, but she figured she could leave out the Rob-Robby-*Robe* part. She glanced in the rearview mirror, pulling back onto the main road. "He told me that Valerie's family *does* know his family." She slowed to a stop at the next intersection. "Well, her dad knows *his* dad, anyway. He made me swear not to tell. . . ."

"C, you know you're gonna tell me. So just get it over with."

"The Packwoods moved out here because of Valerie," Charlotte admitted. "She practically flunked out of her old school, and she had some drama, and she lost all her old friends. . . ." She gunned the accelerator, swept up in a wave of shame and general self-loathing. Summer should not be about spying. It shouldn't be about secrets or suspicion.

Summer should be about hanging around the pool. *Period.* When had it all changed?

"So then why is she stealing Georgia, and Mar — Marcus, and Caleb from us?"

Charlotte shot Brooke a quick glance as she changed lanes. She'd noticed how Brooke had stumbled over Marcus's name. Brooke's hazel eyes seemed to have glazed over, too. Charlotte could see it even in the flickering light of the sunset.

"B?" she said softly, turning her eyes back to the road. "You — you really like Marcus, don't you?"

"We hooked up," Brooke whispered, sounding surprisingly vulnerable.

"Sauna?" Charlotte guessed with a sigh. She knew how Brooke operated by now.

"Sauna," Brooke affirmed, digging around in her clutch for what Charlotte guessed was lip gloss — Brooke's favorite armor. "But what does it matter," she went on furiously, jerking out a tube of Stila. "Clearly he's much more into Valerie — or Georgia."

"And what about Caleb?" Charlotte said quietly. "Who do you think *he's* into?" For the weirdest reason, she felt like she was going to cry.

"Well, one thing's for sure — there's no way in *hell* we're going to Georgia's July Fourth picnic," Brooke announced in response. She shoved the lip gloss back into her bag.

"Oh, come on." Charlotte summoned some composure as she pulled back up to Silver Oaks.

"No. We aren't, Charlotte," she snapped. "Not after what she's done to us."

Charlotte shrunk back in the driver's seat. She wasn't even sure who Brooke *was* right now. She was wearing some other face — a face Charlotte had never seen, not even when Brooke had fallen into a funk over a boy in the past.

"Brooke, I hate to say it, but Marcus Craft isn't worth getting this upset over," she finally murmured.

"What makes you say that?" Brooke shot back.

"I —" Charlotte shrugged. "Forget it." She could feel a fight brewing with Brooke — a bad one. But she didn't want to get into it yet. Better to see where the rest of the summer took them.

Chapter Seventeen

The Tennis Type

Valerie made the suggestion Thursday morning, in the parking lot.

"Hey, G? Instead of playing here at the club today, why don't we try those courts at the state park? Let's slum it."

It was a stroke of genius. *Slumming it.* Georgia didn't hesitate for a second. The two of them immediately loaded Valerie's bike into the trunk of Georgia's SUV, tossed their rackets in the backseat, and hit the road. With the windows rolled down, the wind whipping through their hair, and the radio cranked — some old Rolling Stones song, but still great driving music — Georgia actually felt *free.* They didn't even need to make conversation. What was the point? Valerie had said everything she'd needed to say yesterday, when she'd introduced Marcus, Georgia, and Caleb to her parents.

Georgia still couldn't get over how positive and optimistic Valerie was. She had lost her *life.* That was no exaggeration. For years, she'd gone to a private school in New York, where she'd grown up, where she'd been comfortable and confident — then *poof*! It was all gone, just because she'd gotten lousy grades. Suddenly, Valerie was thrust into a new home, in a new town, with new people to try to befriend . . . and she was dealing with poise and grace.

Valerie's parents were also very cool, as was Valerie's older brother, Sebastian, who also happened to be exceptionally hot (a fact Georgia would have paid closer attention to had Caleb and Marcus not been distracting her).

Amazingly, the courts at the state park weren't all that bad. They were clay, sure, but they weren't scuffed or worn; they were freshly painted and sparkling green. Plus, the nearby forest and rolling hills provided a pretty awesome scenic backdrop, definitely more inviting than a dark, ivy-covered wall. It was also kind of refreshing to see people wearing something other than the Silver Oaks monogram, or even tennis whites. The couple on the next court wore tie-dyes and cut-offs. (Horrors!)

Best of all, though, was the pool — huge and noisy and chaotic, a place where people actually *swam*. And the poor lifeguard had to dive into the pool five separate times in the brief time Georgia and Valerie lounged there, post-tennis. He may not have been as hot as Marcus (he was more a Caleb type), but, unlike Marcus, he was actually doing his job.

"What do you say we come here again tomorrow?" Georgia suggested as they climbed back into her SUV at the end of the afternoon.

Valerie heaved a sigh of relief. "Whew. I thought you'd hate it."

"Are you kidding?"

"Thanks," Valerie said. "And thanks for hanging out with me and the boys yesterday. I feel like it's awkward around Caleb ever since I asked him to the ball."

"Yeah . . . awkward," Georgia echoed, feeling awkward herself. She had told Charlotte about the invite a couple days back, and Charlotte had seemed crushed.

"Georgia, you know that the only reason I asked Caleb was to protect you. I'm not interested in him. I mean, he's sweet . . . but he's not my type. I like the more athletic kind. The tennis type."

The tennis type. Georgia clenched her jaw. *Ethan.* It was inevitable. Leaving Silver Oaks for a day wouldn't somehow transport her to a magical wonderland where she could forget about him. How could it?

"Did I do something wrong?" Valerie asked. "Does Charlotte hate me now?"

Georgia shook her head. "No," she mumbled.

The worst part of the whole situation was that Brooke and Charlotte were practically out of the picture entirely. Georgia hadn't meant to alienate her best friends. It had just sort of happened.

"It'll be awkward if I see Charlotte at Silver Oaks, won't it?" Valerie was saying.

Georgia stuck her key into the ignition. "Valerie, I swear to God, it'll always be awkward at Silver Oaks, even if you're a lifelong member. Why do you think I want to have the July Fourth picnic at my house?"

Valerie glanced at her. "So you don't mind coming here instead? You know, to play tennis?"

"Not only do I not mind, but I'm gonna pick you up at your house tomorrow to play here again." Georgia grabbed the gearshift and pushed it into drive.

After dropping Valerie off at home, Georgia wondered if she should swing by Brooke's or Charlotte's houses. Just like old times — an impromptu visit. But she decided to go home and shower first.

She rounded the corner onto Meadow Lane — the tiny three-house street where she'd grown up, tucked in the woods across town from Silver Oaks. Instantly, she spotted a dark figure standing on her front walk, silhouetted against the glare of the sunset. Her stomach jumped with hope. Maybe Brooke or Charlotte had come to *her*.

It wasn't Brooke or Charlotte, though. It wasn't even Ethan. It was Marcus Craft.

She jerked to a stop. She tried to smile as she hopped out of the car, to hide her discomfiture, but this was just a little too strange. It didn't help that he was wearing a pale green T-shirt that showed off his muscular arms or that his blond hair swept across his face in the late afternoon breeze.

"Hey," she said, slamming the driver's door shut.

He shoved his hands into his pockets. "Hey." Crickets chirped in the falling twilight.

Suddenly, Georgia was very self-conscious of how lousy she looked in a pair of gym shorts and an ancient Yankees T-shirt. Not the most flattering wardrobe.

Marcus turned toward her white-shingled house. His eyes roved over the broad porch, complete with the rope swing, the turret at the end (Georgia lived in the tower), the black shutters, and the sloping roofs. Charlotte always referred to the place as "Martha Stewart" — in other words, *new*, but still tasteful. Brooke never commented on it. Then again, Brooke lived in one of those awful, ultra-modern monstrosities: a maze of glass and wood and white tile — impressive and opulent, but cool and austere. Kind of like Brooke herself.

"Nice place," he remarked.

"Thanks," she said.

"Look, Georgia, I just wanted to tell you that I'm sorry for the way I acted Sunday morning, okay?"

She shook her head. "What way?"

He turned back toward her. "You know, when I was hanging out by the pool with Brooke. What I said about Valerie. That she was a liar. That wasn't cool. I could tell it bummed you out."

Georgia started to smile. "Well, okay, that's fine. But it all worked out anyway, right? I mean we all hung out that afternoon."

He nodded, staring down at his Tevas. He looked just as out of sorts as she *felt*.

"What's wrong, Marcus? If you feel bad, I'm not the one you should be telling. You should be telling Valerie. But I don't even think you need to."

"That's not why I'm here." He stepped closer to her,

the sun dancing off his hair. "I'm here because I care about how *you* feel."

Georgia's breath quickened.

"I know I shouldn't even be saying this," he began, drawing even closer, until his face filled her entire field of vision. "I know the policy, and everything. . . ."

The policy! Georgia's heart squeezed. The policy had already crushed her once. And how about that other policy — the one about not poaching thy friend's love interest? Her thoughts raced. . . . What was Marcus doing? She fought to come up with something to fire back at him, but her brain felt muddled.

He took her hand.

"What about Brooke?" she whispered vacantly. She didn't even feel as if she were *there*: outside her house, on her street, after a long day of tennis. She felt as if she were watching someone else in some other place, listening to someone else talk.

"I like Brooke," Marcus breathed. "But I think I like you more."

Georgia closed her eyes. Even through her dizziness, she could sense him approaching, drawn like a magnet. This time, there was no pushing him away. She gave herself up. She couldn't stop. She began to kiss him, to taste his mouth, his tongue —

She broke away. "I can't," she said, experiencing a horrible déjà vu.

"Georgia, I'm sorry," he whispered. "I —"

"I think you better leave," she said thickly. "This is all

wrong." Before she realized it, her eyes had welled with tears. She turned and fled into her house, slamming the door behind her.

"Georgia!" he shouted after her. "I'm sorry!"

She raced upstairs to her room, where she dove into her bed and buried her face in her pillow for a long, long time.

Later that night, it started to drizzle.

Chapter Eighteen

A Kiss Is Just a Kiss

Maybe Charlotte shouldn't have come to the club in such a funk. The rain certainly didn't improve her mood much. Her brand-new Miu Miu sandals were soaking, and she was forced to make a quick stop in the ladies' room, because her mascara had started to run. Normally, Charlotte didn't wear mascara, but today was special. Kind of.

To add insult to injury, Mom had insisted that Charlotte drag Stella McCartney along, though of course Charlotte refused to bring him inside. Stella could wait in the backseat of the BMW while she took care of this quick matter of business. The dog could also provide a convenient excuse for her to leave.

Charlotte von Klaus was taking control of her life.

Given her weird episode with Brooke in the car, and the fact that Georgia had pretty much fallen off the face of the earth with Valerie, the time had come for Charlotte to fend for herself. She'd just find Caleb, and ask him face-to-face why he'd agreed to go to the Midsummer Ball with Valerie.

After one last check in the bathroom mirror, to make sure her long, red curls were presentable, she marched out and headed toward the billiards room. Her sandals made little squishy noises on the marble. *Ugh.* Hopefully Caleb wouldn't be in the middle of a game right now. But then, he sucked at pool, so the odds were in her favor. He usually sat off to the side while the Robby Miller crew dominated. She could already hear Robby's boisterous laugh.

Charlotte turned the corner, and skidded to a stop. *Whoa.*

For a split-second she stood there, processing the scene. It was unexpected, to say the least. Sure the usual pool boys were there. But Caleb was conspicuously absent. And most unexpected of all was that *Ethan* was there, for once not in his tennis whites . . . and he was with Valerie. As in *with*, with. He stood behind her, guiding her hands as she leaned over the pool table, showing her how to aim the cue. She kept giggling. She was wearing a strapless pink dress that showed off her bronze tan, and she was sort of mashing her butt against Ethan's body as she pretended to try to shoot the ball.

Charlotte blinked. She took a few steps back and then rounded the corner, leaning against the wall. Weirdly, she felt a sudden, relieved warmth welling up inside her.

So. Valerie wasn't interested in Caleb. Nor was she interested in Marcus. She was interested in *Ethan*. Not that this was good, per se. It sucked for Georgia; that was for sure. So . . . why couldn't Charlotte stop smiling?

Maybe she knew why. She wasn't quite ready to acknowledge it yet, but Charlotte wondered if she maybe kind of almost wanted to kiss Caleb again. That Spin the Bottle game had been one thing, but then that time in the bar in DC . . . something about Caleb's kisses made Charlotte's heart sing. So she didn't want him kissing Valerie. Or anyone else, for that matter. At all.

Not sure why she was doing what she was doing, Charlotte dug through her bag and fished out her new pink Moto Razr (a divorce-guilt gift from Dad). She took a deep breath, programmed the picture-snapping option, and kicked off her sandals as to avoid any squeaking or squishing. She'd have to make this fast. . . . *Three, two, one — Go!* In a single move, she ducked low around the corner, snapped a quick picture of Ethan and Valerie snuggling over their pool game, then jammed her feet back into her sandals and bolted down the hall. Her sandals smacked on the floor, and she held her breath, hoping no one had seen —

"Yo, Charlotte! Wait up! Where're you running off to?"

Great.

She sighed and turned. Robby Miller waved from the far end of the hall. "I thought I saw you. Come here." He turned his baseball cap backward, straightening his white T-shirt. "I was just talking about you."

Charlotte shot a quick glance toward the door. "I — I really need to get back to my car, Robby. Stella is waiting for me."

Robby smirked, swaggering down the hall toward her. "You don't want to hear what I was saying about you?"

In spite of herself, Charlotte grinned. Robby actually

looked . . . well, sort of cute tonight. At least he didn't look like he was auditioning for a Wu-Tang reunion video.

Charlotte crossed her arms over her chest, still clutching her cell phone. "All right, Robby. What did you say?"

His smile widened as he glanced down at her purple toenails. He stopped in front of her and raised his eyes.

"I was *saying* . . . that there are no real chicks at this country club."

Charlotte burst out laughing. She couldn't help it. "Well, gee, Robby. Thanks so much. You really know how to sweet-talk a lady. If the chicks here are so heinous, why don't you just go back to Kenwood?"

He pursed his lips and shook his head. "Nah, woman — you gotta let me finish. For one thing, the chicks at Kenwood are all skanks. Not like you."

Charlotte shook her head. "Excuse me?"

"Listen up." He lowered his voice, glancing back over his shoulder toward the billiards room. "I know Valerie thinks she's all that. Just because she's fine. But you're *real*, girl. You're a thousand times better than her. I was talking to Johnny about this exact thing. I'm just sick of these chicks with egos, know what I'm sayin'?"

Charlotte felt her face flushing with pleasure at Robby's words, and he held her gaze, smiling at her. She remembered how he'd struck her as surprisingly insightful during their impromptu lunch together, and now she once again felt a swell of fondness toward him. She'd known Robby Miller forever — almost as long as she'd known Caleb — but, unlike Caleb, Robby had never stood out from the crowd, never struck Charlotte as anything other than a typical pool boy. But this summer, everything was different. Charlotte suddenly felt like she'd grown a new pair of eyes, and was seeing everyone — Brooke, Georgia, Caleb — as if she'd never known any of them before. Which was kind of freaky — and might warrant an extra session with Dr. Gilmore.

But right now all Charlotte saw was Robby. Her lingering confusion over Caleb, the sense of flattery that was washing over her, and the undeniable adorableness of Robby's crooked smile all came together at once, making Charlotte's stomach jump and her feet move, impossibly, toward Robby.

"You don't need to . . ." she told him shakily. "I mean . . . you don't have to say those things."

Robby shrugged one shoulder. "Hey, I'm serious, Charlotte." He glanced down, seeming to drop his usual bravado. "Just . . . thought I'd tell you."

"Well, thanks, Robby." Feeling bold and crazy and a little *why-not?*, Charlotte came even closer to him and planted a kiss on his surprisingly warm, smooth cheek. Before she could pull back, though, Robby rested a hand on her arm. Their eyes met briefly and then, suddenly, she and Robby Miller were kissing. *Really* kissing. There they stood, their arms sliding around each other, in the hall outside the billiards room of Silver Oaks, where anyone — Ethan, Valerie — could come out to find them. But Charlotte didn't care. Kissing Robby didn't feel as *right* as kissing Caleb — Robby's style was a little aggressive for her tastes — but she was still loving the feel of it.

Then, as Robby moved his hand slowly down her back, and his lips slid off her mouth down toward her neck, Charlotte realized they were moving from *kissing* mode to *making out* mode, and there was definitely a difference.

She drew back, catching her breath, and Robby stared at her, looking as shocked as she felt.

"I — shouldn't —" Charlotte tried to get the words out, but Robby shook his head.

"Charlotte, it's okay —" Robby said, taking a step toward her.

"I have to go," Charlotte mumbled. "Stella — Stella's waiting in the car. . . ."

And with that, Charlotte spun around and fled toward the door. She burst outside, into the pouring rain, and ran in her noisy sandals to her car. Her heart felt as if it would pop right out of her chest. Hunching her shoulders against the cold raindrops, she fumbled with her keys, finally unlocking the door and sliding inside. Stella was whining on the backseat. He scrambled up as soon as Charlotte got in the car, distressed at having been left alone for so long with nothing to watch but the rain.

Charlotte tried to take deep, calming breaths. *Why did I do that?* She'd just been thinking about how much she liked kissing *Caleb*. . . . Was that why she'd randomly attacked Robby Miller? And, yes, he'd kissed her back. But . . .

Nothing made sense.

Charlotte noticed that she was still gripping her cell phone in her fist. Suddenly, she remembered the picture of Ethan and Valerie and wanted to burst out laughing. What was *with* her tonight? Ducking around taking furtive photos, kissing boys out of nowhere?

At least there was one thing Charlotte knew she could do, she thought as she petted a distraught Stella and then turned the key in the ignition. She was going straight to Brooke's house to show her the picture. Charlotte didn't want Georgia to see the cruel evidence, but maybe Brooke could shed some light on the situation.

Charlotte only hoped she wouldn't be stirring up more trouble.

Chapter Nineteen

The Uglifier

I broke an Unspoken Rule.

Georgia stared at herself in the cabana bathroom mirror. Rain thudded on the roof — a hard, steady, summer rain. Night had melted into morning, and Georgia had finally summoned the courage to drive to Silver Oaks. She'd secretly hoped Valerie would be there. But her new buddy was spending the day with her brother, Sebastian. So now Georgia was left hiding out in the cabana when, according to *another* Unspoken Rule, she should have been hanging out in the billiards room with her two best friends.

She'd spent most of last night sobbing into her pillow, and this morning, she still felt like a zombie. Too bad the nightmarish, fluorescent cabana light didn't improve her mood much. Eons ago, she and Brooke and Charlotte had even coined a name for it: "the Uglifier." But then, Georgia would have looked ugly to herself no matter where she was. She couldn't understand what Marcus — or any guy — could see in her.

And why couldn't this goddamn rain ever stop?

I just have to tell Brooke the truth, Georgia decided. She sniffled and rubbed her eyes, then ran a hand through her hair. She smoothed her green Tommy Hilfiger tank and tugged on her linen A-line skirt. *It's not that big a deal, is it? Maybe she's already over him. Or not.*

The worst part was that Georgia didn't trust Marcus. He was a good kisser, yes, but so were most players. And she didn't want Brooke getting hurt by him in the end.

Thank God Ethan got the day off when it rained. She knew she couldn't deal with bumping into him right now. But she also knew she couldn't hide in the cabana forever. Eventually, she'd have to emerge and find Brooke.

"Georgia?"

And speak of the devil.

"Hey," Georgia breathed.

Brooke stood in the bathroom doorway, dripping with rain. For once, she wasn't coiffed and made-up. Her black hair was in disarray — and she was wearing *sneakers*. (Metallic Pumas, yes, but still.) She'd also thrown on an old Silver Oaks windbreaker, one she hadn't worn in a very long time. Georgia almost smiled. Two summers ago, on a rainy day like today, in a fit of juvenile regression and boredom, Georgia, Brooke, and Charlotte had taken turns scribbling dumb, snarky little phrases in eyeliner next to the silver *S.O.* monogram, and then scrubbing them off. *S.O.* YESTERDAY . . . *S.O.* NOT COOL . . . *S.O.* WHAT? . . . Eventually they'd damaged the waterproof nylon. Georgia could still see a dark stain to the right of the letters.

"You're a hard person to track down these days,"

Brooke stated coldly. "I've barely seen you since the season started."

Georgia swallowed. "I know, Brooke. I'm sorry."

"Why are you hanging out with Marcus and Valerie 24/7?"

Georgia clenched her fists at her sides. The vow she'd made to be honest with Brooke about the Marcus situation slipped away as quickly as she'd made it, and for no logical reason she could explain. All she knew was that she didn't feel sad or guilty anymore. She felt trapped and angry and accused, and pulled in about a dozen different directions.

"Georgia, is this about Ethan?" Brooke asked, softening her tone. She avoided Georgia's gaze, choosing to stare at her friendship bracelet instead. "I know that you still like him. So there's something I need to tell you about him and Valerie."

"What are you talking about?" Georgia's heart froze.

Brooke tucked a damp strand of hair behind her ear. "Valerie's into him," she said. "And I can prove it."

Georgia rolled her eyes. She almost laughed. She'd always known Brooke was manipulative, but she'd never imagined she would out-and-out lie. "Brooke, please. Give it up."

"Whatever. I'm just saying that you should talk to Charlotte. She has some information you might find interesting."

"Well, what if I don't *want* to talk to Charlotte?"

Georgia took a deep breath and stepped away from the mirror. "Listen, it's fine that you and Charlotte like to create drama wherever you go. I respect that. But *I'm* not like that. Okay?"

Brooke withdrew, clearly stung. "I'm not creating drama," she breathed.

Georgia's lips trembled. "You want to know something?" She felt as if she were standing outside herself, watching someone else. "Valerie actually thinks you're cool. She wants to get to know you — and Charlotte. But you guys are *so* exclusive —"

"Well, maybe we'd be nicer to her if she stopped throwing herself at every boy in Silver Oaks —" Brooke began in her iciest voice.

"Look, she's not interested in Marcus, okay?" Georgia cut Brooke off. Saying his name made her limbs shake, but she tried to remain firm. "And I don't think he's interested in her."

"What makes you so sure?" Brooke challenged, but Georgia thought she could see a glimmer of hope in her hazel eyes. That made Georgia feel even worse.

"I — I don't want to talk about it now," Georgia said, spinning around to face the mirror. She felt on the verge of bursting into tears, but she hated to let Brooke see her break down.

"Fine," Brooke snapped, and in her peripheral vision Georgia could see her turning away. "So maybe we shouldn't talk anymore. . . . Period."

"Fine," Georgia echoed, her voice coming out trembly.

She shut her eyes and waited until she heard Brooke stomp away, her sneakers squeaking on the linoleum.

Georgia opened her eyes and stared at her bleak reflection in the mirror. She felt awful having spoken to Brooke like that, but what bothered her the most about their argument was the tiny, niggling seed of doubt Brooke had planted.

What if Valerie *was* into Ethan? And what if he was into her, too? And if so, was there anything on earth Georgia could do about it?

Chapter Twenty

The New Routine

"Who cares?"

Brooke asked this lame question far too often lately. As the hours and days and eventually *weeks* progressed, it became an all-purpose catchphrase — the only way Brooke could get Charlotte to shut up about the whole Georgia situation.

Georgia hadn't shown up at the club once since that rainy day. Not in two whole weeks. It was insane. Aside from two vacations to Europe, none of them had ever gone so long without communicating at least via e-mail.

So when Charlotte tapped Brooke on the shoulder the morning of July Fourth to announce that she'd finally received a text message from Georgia, Brooke didn't even bother to look up from her magazine. She stretched out in the lounger, keeping her eyes firmly fixed on a Fiorucci spread in *Vogue*.

"Who cares?" she said again.

Charlotte shoved her phone in front of Brooke's face.

HEY C ARE U COMING TO THE PICNIC SORRY IVE BEEN SO OUT OF TOUCH. G

Brooke snickered. "So she's alive." Could it be any more *offensive*? It would take a lot more than a half-assed text message to set things straight.

"So what do you say?" Charlotte asked. "You want to go?"

Brooke slammed her *Vogue* shut and tossed it down onto the patio. She glared at Charlotte over the rims of her sunglasses. "You've got to be kidding," she stated.

Charlotte sighed. Her eyes wandered over to Robby Miller and his posse, playing poker under the umbrella nearest to the diving board, and Brooke saw her cheeks color. Why? Charlotte quickly turned back to Brooke. "I don't know, B," she said, twirling her hair with her fingers. "I don't feel like hanging around here, you know?"

Brooke glanced up at Marcus, slouched in the lifeguard chair. With his broad shoulders and muscular arms silhouetted against the overcast sky, he looked like something out of one of those movies about ancient warriors, like *Troy*. He shot her a grin, his eyes teasing. They'd been hooking up off and on in the sauna for a couple weeks now.

"No, C," she murmured happily. "I don't know."

The truth was, Brooke was sort of secretly wishing that Charlotte would get lost. She wanted to fit in some alone time with Marcus in the downstairs sauna before the dumb Fourth of July festivities began. (Last night, her dad informed her that the usual picnic was canceled: It was supposed to rain. Instead, there would be an "indoor luncheon.") Charlotte seemed incapable of taking the hint, though.

Oh, great. And now here comes Ethan.

He slouched toward them, smiling forlornly. He looked scruffier than usual. He probably hadn't shaved in two weeks.

"Hey, you haven't seen Georgia around, have you?" he asked.

Brooke shook her head.

"I don't think she's coming today," Charlotte answered.

"Oh." He mustered a weak laugh. "Well. I guess you guys are more of a duo than a trio of backup singers now," he joked. He turned and headed for the cabana.

"That was a dumb thing to say," Brooke muttered under her breath.

"Don't worry, B," Charlotte said. "We're still like a trio of backup singers. Sometimes they have little squabbles, though, you know? I mean you saw that movie about Tina Turner, right? The one with Angela Basset? Remember how she fought with *her* backup singers?"

Brooke reached for her *Vogue* again. "No. I don't."

As if on cue, a few drops of rain began to fall. Brooke flopped back on her cushions and groaned. Wonderful. Now Marcus would have to busy himself with closing the pool. No way could she get him down into the sauna. All at once, Brooke couldn't help but feel the need to leave Silver Oaks, too — as opposed to retiring to the billiards room and watching the moronic shenanigans of the Robby Miller Posse.

Charlotte's phone began to buzz again.

"Georgia," she said, flipping it open. She held up the little screen for Brooke to see.

HEY C THE PICNIC IS CANCELED CUZ OF THE RAIN.
CALL U LATER.

Brooke let herself fume for a second over the fact that Georgia was still in touch with Charlotte and not her. Then she glanced over at Marcus. He was already working his way down the lifeguard ladder. He flashed a rueful smile.

"Let's go shopping," Charlotte said. "There are always tons of Fourth of July sample sales."

Brooke sighed. "Why not? Maybe I'll get lucky and find something really great. Lord knows I won't get lucky here."

After picking up some Lucky jeans and Mella flip-flops at the mall, the girls drove to the state park to kill time — anything to avoid going back to the club, and each for their own reasons. . . .

When they got there, though, they saw Georgia and Valerie, playing tennis in the rain.

Brooke and Charlotte sat in their seats, with the rain crashing down, speechless. Georgia and Valerie were playing all by themselves in the downpour, swatting a tennis ball back and forth in soaked gym shorts and tees, laughing hysterically like a couple of kindergartners.

And that wasn't the worst part. The worst part was that when Georgia paused to wipe her damp hair off her forehead, Brooke could see that Georgia was missing something: her friendship bracelet. She'd taken it off. She'd violated the sixth Unspoken Rule, the rule she'd inscribed herself. *Don't Toss Out Anything of Value.*

"Let's get out of here," Charlotte mumbled, reading Brooke's mind. "Maybe we can still make the stupid luncheon at the club."

Tires screeching, Charlotte's car spun out of the parking lot and onto the highway. The windshield wipers slapped in an off-kilter rhythm, drowning out the radio.

"Can I ask you something?" Brooke said.

"Sure."

"What did Dr. Gilmore say about Georgia, you know, ditching us and all that?"

Charlotte lifted her shoulders. "He says that we're all stressed about colleges and stuff. He says that we all could be 'acting out.'"

Brooke frowned. "But we haven't even started *applying* to colleges yet."

"Yeah, but we will pretty soon." Charlotte sighed. "He says that sometimes people drift apart. Especially if they've been close as kids —" She bit her lip. Her grip tightened on the wheel, her knuckles whitening. "Whatever. He's just a stupid shrink who wears a bow tie. It's not like he has any idea of what's really going on."

For once in her life, Brooke didn't have a dry or witty comeback. "You think G will at least come to the Midsummer Ball?" she heard herself ask. "I know we've joked about it and even said a few times that we wouldn't go. But at least we were going to go shopping for it."

Charlotte shrugged again. "Honestly, your guess is as good as mine," she answered quietly.

"Yeah, well, whatever." Brooke sighed. "Who cares?"

* * *

The Fourth of July came and went without much activity, but the very next day, Brooke finally got the fireworks she'd been craving.

The day dawned brilliantly — perfect suntanning weather — and at the pool that morning, Marcus caught her eye and gave her a long, knowing look. Brooke smiled back, and that afternoon, they met up in the sauna.

"It's been a while," Brooke murmured, letting her pool robe drop as Marcus walked over to her. She'd missed him so much, but she didn't want to let on.

"Yeah," Marcus replied with a grin, undoing the strings on her halter bikini. He leaned in and started kissing her. His lips were warm and salty; his tongue was insistent. Brooke responded in kind, and soon the two of them were down on the bench, going at it like crazy.

"Hang on," Marcus whispered, pulling back to catch his breath. "There's — um — before we get too busy, there's something I've been wanting to ask you."

"What?" Brooke drew back, too. She met Marcus's wide blue eyes. *About Georgia? Or Valerie?* She didn't know what to expect anymore.

"It's about the Midsummer Ball," Marcus whispered, tracing a pattern on Brooke's bare shoulder with his finger. "I know the girls who are getting inducted generally have escorts or whatever, so I was wondering if I could be yours?" He gave her a winning smile.

"You — what?" Brooke whispered back in disbelief. Maybe she and Marcus *weren't* just about random hookups.

Maybe he did want something more. But was the Midsummer Ball really the appropriate venue to take her relationship with Marcus to the next level? He was an employee, after all. Wouldn't her dad utterly lose his shit?

And why would that be so bad?

Before Brooke could respond to Marcus either way, her cell phone, which she'd tucked into the pocket of her pool robe, began buzzing loudly. Retying the strings of her halter, Brooke bent down and plucked out the phone. It was Charlotte.

"Do you need to take that?" Marcus asked, standing up and stretching. "I can wait outside if you want."

"Yeah . . . I should get it," Brooke said. It wasn't like Charlotte to call in the middle of the day, so Brooke knew something had to be up.

Marcus promised Brooke he'd be waiting outside, and then ambled out of the sauna room, leaving her alone with her cell.

"C, you'll never guess," Brooke said immediately. "Marcus invited me to the Midsummer Ball. The invitation bug seems to be catching."

There was a pause. "Interesting," Charlotte said flatly. "Have fun."

Brooke clenched the phone in her slick fingers, annoyed. "C? I gotta tell you, I'm not in the mood for mind games right now. What's going on?"

Charlotte laughed. "Oh, nothing. Just that now, everybody officially has a date to the Midsummer Ball except me. Ethan is going with Georgia. You're going with

Marcus. And Caleb is going with Valerie. Maybe you guys should all get a hotel room together or something."

Brooke held her breath, waiting for the follow-up.

"Did you hear me?" Charlotte asked.

"Yeah, I heard you," Brooke said irritably. "It's a joke, right?"

"No, it's not a joke. Jesus, B, can't you think about somebody besides yourself for once?" Charlotte demanded.

Brooke opened her mouth, but no words would come.

"Hey, I'm sorry, okay?" Charlotte mumbled in the silence. "Don't worry about me. Honestly. You never do, anyway."

"C —"

"I gotta go."

Click.

Brooke stared at the phone. The first thought that leaped to her mind was: *Charlotte's on the verge of another breakdown, and I have to talk to Georgia right away.* She punched in the speed-dial and brought the phone back to her ear.

After two rings, Georgia answered. "Hello?" she said softly, her voice incredulous. "Brooke?"

Brooke drew in a deep breath, steeled her nerves, and plunged straight in. "G, listen," she began. "I know we're —"

"I'm not interested in Marcus, Brooke, I swear," Georgia interrupted. "I was just confused, and upset, and you were right; it's more about Ethan."

Brooke blinked, scowling. "What?"

"Marcus told you, didn't he? That's why I've been staying away from the club. I didn't want to see him. I wanted him to be with *you*."

"What are you talking about?" Brooke demanded, her blood running cold.

"Marcus didn't tell you?"

"Tell me *what*?"

Georgia was silent.

"G, what was Marcus supposed to tell me?"

"That he kissed me."

Brooke didn't answer. The tiny sauna bench seemed to crumble beneath her and send her free-falling into a bottomless abyss. She couldn't believe Marcus was still waiting outside. Well, let him wait. Forever. She'd walk by him, freeze him out.

"Brooke? Are you there? It was just one time — and — um —"

"No, G. He didn't tell me about it. But just so you know, Charlotte is really pissed off, and I think the three of us should meet."

"I . . . uh, okay. Yeah. Let's meet. How about the golf course, around seven P.M.? Let's say the thirteenth hole. I'll call Charlotte."

"Valerie's not invited, is she?" Brooke asked frostily.

"Of course not. B, come on —"

"Done."

Chapter Twenty-One

13th-Hole Séance

Georgia never understood why the die-hard golfers didn't play at this hour. It was the most beautiful time of day — the sun sinking, the wind picking up, the sky golden red in the west and dark blue in the east. But then, the diehard golfers liked to drink cocktails at this hour. And given the sub-zero expression on Brooke's face, and the way Charlotte was furiously twirling her red hair, well, some cocktails right now might have been a good idea.

"So, we're all here," Georgia announced. She watched her two (former?) best friends pace the green. "Let's talk. Or let's at least try to conjure John Lennon."

Brooke froze in her tracks. "That's not funny," she said.

"Oh, come on, B," Charlotte groaned. "Let's just please —"

"Let's just please *what*?" Brooke snapped. "Georgia is making fun of you, Charlotte. But I guess I shouldn't be surprised. The 'nice' Georgia Palmer we knew is gone. Either she's cloned herself, or she's had one of those face transplants."

"Brooke, *relax*, all right?" Charlotte pleaded, her voice rising. "I don't care if Georgia is making fun of me."

Charlotte marched over and planted herself between the two of them, her red curls bright in the twilight. "Georgia can say what she wants. I mean, *I* could say a lot of stuff right now. But I don't want to hurt anyone's feelings." Charlotte gave Brooke a pointed stare.

Brooke laughed. "Oh, please. What? Are you talking about that picture you —"

"Shut up, B," Charlotte hissed.

Georgia glowered at Brooke. "What are you talking about?"

"Nothing, Georgia. So you did try to poach Marcus?" Brooke asked demurely, affecting an air of fake innocence.

Charlotte winced.

"Brooke, I apologized for that," Georgia whispered, clenching her jaw.

"Exactly!" Charlotte exclaimed, before either of them could say another word.

Georgia's eyes bored into Brooke's. Brooke stared down at her Manolos. "What picture?" Georgia asked.

"Look, everybody here kisses tons of other people," Charlotte babbled. "It's practically Silver Oaks tradition. Take my own parents —"

"C, cut out the stand-up routine tonight, okay?" Brooke moaned. "It loses its charm fast. This is serious."

Charlotte whirled and stared at Brooke. "You know, we wouldn't even be fighting right now if it weren't for Valerie," she spat.

"Valerie?" Georgia asked, not sure if Charlotte was joking again.

"Yes," Charlotte replied. "Valerie." She kept her eyes on Brooke.

Georgia threw her hands in the air. "This has nothing to *do* with Valerie!"

"It has everything to do with Valerie!" Brooke and Charlotte cried at the exact same time, spinning to face her.

"Funny." Georgia shook her head, now more angry than miserable. "This is just what I was talking about — with Valerie herself."

Brooke rolled her eyes. "What's that, G?"

"It's just . . . It's almost, like, psychic. That you two have this connection. And sometimes it gets pretty annoying. That's all. I guess it's just taken me a long time to come out and say it."

Brooke stepped forward, brushing Charlotte aside. "G, that's not cool."

"What isn't?" she demanded.

"I just . . . this isn't like — it isn't like you," Brooke said — actually stammering, which she never did. "We *all* have that connection. Has there ever been a summer — other than this one — when we haven't hung out together? I mean, yeah, you've always liked spending more time playing tennis than hanging out with us by the pool, but —"

"Excuse me? Why do you keep saying I'm not like *myself*?" Georgia was simmering now. Brooke's comment wasn't a compliment or a confession or even an attempt to help; it was a not-so-veiled snub, nearly identical to Ethan's — and it perfectly summed up everything that had driven Georgia crazy recently. "Maybe you never knew me in the first place. And you're right — I *do* like playing tennis more than hanging out by the pool and listening to your inane gossip. I mean, come on, Brooke! You spotted Marcus and you *called* him, like you were calling first dibs on a new pair of Sevens. You're shallow, Brooke Farnsworth."

Charlotte stepped between them again, extending a hand to each. "This is so stupid, you guys. There's no way I'm gonna let this happen."

"Well, it *is* happening," Brooke shot back. "Deal with it. Maybe the three of us are just growing apart."

Charlotte shook her head, her face registering shock, and Georgia felt a similar pang of surprised sadness. But, somehow she found her voice.

"Maybe we grew apart a long time ago," Georgia whispered. "Maybe we've been playing a charade of friendship all along."

"Well, true friends wouldn't act the way we've been acting all summer," Charlotte acknowledged, swallowing hard.

This is like a séance, Georgia realized. Only this time the girls were dredging up the ghosts of their pasts.

"Fine," Brooke said icily. "Then if the point of coming here was to be honest, here's *my* honest opinion — I wouldn't mind never seeing either of you again."

"Gee, my sentiments exactly," Charlotte snapped. Then, looking as if she were going to cry, she turned and dashed across the green. Georgia watched her go. Her stomach squeezed. For the first time in her life, she had an idea of how crazy, and neurotic, and sad Charlotte must have felt all the time. So she decided to follow her example. She ran away from Brooke, too — but in the opposite direction.

And, as Georgia darted across the lawn in the setting sun, she caught a glimpse of two figures, laughing and talking beside the ivy walls of the tennis court. Two figures that made her heart stop.

They were Ethan and Valerie.

Chapter Twenty-Two

Freaking Out

Two hours later, after some important errands and a visit home to change, Charlotte strolled toward the club's main entrance, her Jimmy Choo heels clattering. It was dinnertime.

She paused, digging into her black velvet handbag to fish out a newly purchased pack of American Spirit cigarettes and a lighter. It was funny; buying cigarettes was harder than she'd thought. She'd actually been carded at the gas station. After batting her eyelashes and pleading in the ditziest, sluttiest voice she could muster ("Come on, sweetie, they're not even for *me*!") the pimply attendant sold her the pack in spite of her age, probably because he was even younger than *she* was.

Her hands trembling slightly, she stuck a cigarette in her mouth and flicked the lighter. *Yikes*. The flame nearly singed her eyebrows. She'd only smoked one other time in her life — coincidentally (or not), the night she'd slugged that Pinot Noir straight from the bottle. Brooke had joined her for the smoking portion of the evening and promptly turned green after three puffs. Charlotte herself had coughed for about twenty minutes and felt nauseated long afterward, so she'd learned her lesson: *Don't inhale.* Good thing she'd decided to slug some Merlot back home tonight. And that her mom had offered to drop her off at the Club before she went to her evening yogalates class.

Charlotte was actually pretty tipsy. Whatever. The wine had matched her lip gloss.

She sucked furiously, cigar-style, until a cloud of smoke enveloped her. Perfect.

With the lit cigarette dangling from her heavily glossed lips, she kicked her Jimmy Choos into the planter next to the doorway. She doubted anyone would notice them there. And if someone did swipe them . . . Well, whatever. They were from the Fall 2004 line. No big loss.

"Silver Oaks, get ready," she said out loud.

She flicked some burning ashes onto the ground and pushed through the doors, padding swiftly through the cold marble hallway in her bare feet. She caught a few gaping stares from some of the parlor crowd. *What's the matter, boys? You've never seen a shoeless, fiery she-demon before? Haven't you heard that the devil wears Prada?*

Her pulse raced as she approached the closed dining room door. Charlotte didn't know *what* she was going to do at dinner tonight, but making a scene was definitely going to be part of it.

With a final exhalation of the foul-tasting smoke, Charlotte threw open the dining room doors and stepped inside, coughing loudly.

She wasn't sure what to expect, but dead calm wasn't on her list of scenarios.

She found a room full of mummies. Literally. It looked as if they had all been embalmed and frozen in place. Nobody even seemed particularly disturbed by her sudden, smoky entrance. Maybe a dozen or so of the usual crowd were eating dinner, dressed in their casual evening wear: Georgia's parents, Brooke's parents, Robby Miller's parents . . . Charlotte was sick of the monotony. It was time to *really* mix things up.

She marched over to the bar and extinguished her cigarette in Marcia Palmer's glass of Chardonnay. (Finally, that elicited *some* reaction. It wasn't quite a gasp, more of a shocked whimper, but still audible.) Then she planted a kiss on Jimmy the Bartender's cheek as he poured a vodka and cranberry. And when Mrs. Miller shot her a disgusted look, Charlotte stuck her tongue out at her. So much for "respect and decorum."

"Charlotte von Klaus, what in God's name do you think you're doing?" Mr. Farnsworth barked, approaching her.

Charlotte had never really appreciated until this moment how much Brooke resembled her father: the same black hair, the same flawless, porcelain complexion — the same heartless cruelty. She inched toward the patio doors, smiling back at him. She was no longer nervous. No, she felt an extraordinary, almost mystical calm.

"Well, young lady?" he demanded.

"I had an eye-opening chat with your daughter this evening," Charlotte replied. "And I realized how little *any* of you mean to me."

Mr. Farnsworth's jaw twitched. He reached into his

inside blazer pocket and snatched out his cell phone, then began furiously punching in a number.

"If you're trying to call my mom, I wouldn't bother," Charlotte said, pushing open the patio doors. "She's not home."

"Where do you think you're going?" he shouted after her.

"I'm going for a swim, Mr. Farnsworth. The pool's still open, isn't it?" She shut the doors behind her — and nearly slammed right into Robby Miller.

"Damn, girl!" Robby said. "What's gotten into *you*?"

It took a moment for Charlotte to catch her breath. It took another few seconds for her eyes to adjust to the dim light of the bug torches on the patio, and her heart began to pound. She hadn't seen Robby since their mini-make-out session.

But she was too tipsy to get fluttery.

"*Ro-o-o-be*, thank heavens I've found you," she murmured, in a dead-on impersonation of Audrey Hepburn, circa *Breakfast at Tiffany's*. She draped her arm over his shoulder and ran her fingers through his spiky hair. "You're the only one who understands me."

Robby's lips spread in a gentle smile. "C, are you drunk? Did you take something? You can tell me, I won't care."

"I'm a *little* drunk," Charlotte admitted, shivering. If she stayed out here any longer, she might burst into tears. Robby Miller was being chivalrous. Robby Miller was *not* supposed to be chivalrous. He was supposed to be a stupid pool boy.

Robby reached into his shorts pocket and pulled out his cell phone.

"Who are you calling?" she asked.

He didn't answer right away. He turned away and lowered his voice. "Hey, Caleb?" he said. "It's Rob. Rob Miller. Dude, I'm not bothering you right now, am I? Cool. Here's the thing. I'm a little worried about Charlotte. . . ."

Charlotte had heard enough. Without thinking, she reached down and pulled her strapless dress over her head. In just her bra and panties, she crossed her arms over her chest, tore across the patio, and dove into the pool.

Breathe, stroke, kick . . . Breathe, stroke, kick . . .

After ten haphazard laps, Charlotte began to wonder if Brooke's father and the rest of the dining room crowd had just decided to leave her here to drown. For somebody who prized her solitude, Charlotte was also beginning to see the reality of the sitch: She was a crazy von Klaus, half naked and alone in the pool at the club where she didn't belong, and would probably never be welcome again. Even Robby had split. And on top of it all, she was starting to get cold.

She paused at the shallow end.

Wait a second. Her heart leaped.

A skinny shadow appeared in the patio doors. It was Caleb. She held her breath and listened.

"Let me handle it, Mr. Farnsworth, okay?" Caleb was hissing. "Please. If I can't get her out of here in five minutes, fine. Yes. You can call security. I'd just rather not cause a scene, okay? Just let me try. Thank you."

Security? Now that was funny. Silver Oaks Security consisted of exactly two extremely large middle-aged men, both of whom were named (of all things) Van. One was pasty, and the other was swarthy, and Georgia, Brooke, and Charlotte called them the Motorcycle Twins — after those two obese brothers from the *Guinness Book of World Records.* Charlotte very much doubted they'd be able to help out in this situation.

The patio doors slammed.

Charlotte squinted at Caleb's fuzzy form. (Next time she went swimming, she'd definitely have to wear goggles. Although that raised a very good question: *Where* would she go swimming next time?) He marched toward her and sat at the edge of the closest lounger, then started to untie his sneakers.

"Hey, Caleb," she said. "What are you doing?"

"I'm taking off my clothes. Skinny dipping isn't very much fun alone."

Charlotte glanced back toward the dining room. Several members peered back at her through the glass doors. "Always with the punchy one-liners. Can I ask why?"

Caleb ignored her. He pulled off his sweater and T-shirt, and then began to unbuckle his belt. He shoved his jeans down his legs, revealing swimming trunks instead of boxers.

"Hey, you came prepared!" she exclaimed.

"I was actually hoping you'd get out and let me off the

hook," he said, stepping out of his jeans. "But I wanted to be ready for anything. When Robby called, I got a little nervous. So I'm happy to run and grab us some towels and robes, okay? Then you can change, and I'll drive you home."

"Robe's a nice guy, isn't he?" Charlotte said absently, bending her knees and easing down into the water up to her neck.

"Robe?"

"Rob. Robby Miller."

"Oh, yeah. He sure is. Lousy poker player, but hell of a guy." Caleb sighed. "Now do I need to dive in there and drag you out?"

Charlotte sank farther, blowing some bubbles with her mouth. "I really have to practice my swimming, as you know. The Tombs won't let me graduate if I can't pass the test."

Caleb shook his head. "Charlotte —"

"Just a few more laps, okay?" She prepared to submerge again, but then Caleb dove in after her.

"Where do you think you're going?" he whispered, grabbing her arms. "You can't stay in here forever, C."

She blinked up at him. His soft, dark eyes glistened as water dripped from his black hair. A doleful smile played on his lips.

And that's when it happened: The floodgates opened.

She knew she was bound to start bawling sooner or later. She'd just hoped she'd be able to hold back until she got home.

"It's okay, Charlotte," Caleb soothed, drawing her against him and holding her closely. "Don't cry. Or cry if you want. Just come with me, all right? We'll go to the cabana and dry you off, and then we'll go home."

"I'm sorry, Caleb," she gasped, fighting to catch her breath. She sniffed and buried her face in the crook of his shoulder. "I'm so sorry to put you through this."

"Put me through what?" he asked gently.

"Embarrassing you like this in front of everyone, just because I decided to throw a stupid tantrum."

He chuckled, stroking her wet curls. "You think I'm embarrassed? You actually think I give a crap what they think? To be honest, I'm psyched they're all watching us right now. I hope they *do* call the Motorcycle Twins. Maybe we could all have an extremely low-speed chase across the golf course."

Charlotte laughed through her tears. "Thanks," she croaked.

"For what?"

"For everything. For not taking me for granted."

Caleb pulled away and lifted her chin. "How could I ever take you for granted, Charlotte?"

"Well, I don't know," Charlotte replied tremblingly, suddenly all too aware of how Caleb had spoken her name. And of how he was gazing at her. With undisguised, unabashed tenderness. And desire. "Because I'm a . . . freak?"

"You're not a freak," Caleb murmured, now running one finger along Charlotte's damp cheek. "You just wear your heart on your sleeve. Nothing wrong with that."

"I'm not wearing sleeves," Charlotte mumbled. But before she could continue the joke, Caleb was kissing her. Suddenly, she was back in sixth grade, playing Spin the Bottle, and discovering what a boy's lips felt like for the first time. And then she was on that class trip, kissing Caleb for the second time in her life and wondering what the hell she was doing. But in the next heartbeat, all those memories disappeared, and Charlotte gave herself over to the moment: She and Caleb together, in the pool. Caleb's lithe body wrapped around hers, his long, sweet kisses growing more fervent. Water dripped from Charlotte's fingers as she caressed his cheek. Caleb buried his head in Charlotte's neck. Their legs tangled under the surface. This was real. This was now. And this was right.

Caleb drew back for a second to smile at her, and Charlotte caught her breath, but then she sought his mouth with hers again. And she knew then, as she melted in his arms, that there was one part of her heart she *hadn't* worn on her sleeve: the part that belonged to Caleb. Her feelings for him were bigger than any of her problems, bigger than the possibility of getting kicked out of the club. None of that mattered now. All that mattered was their kiss, which, in the cool water and under the sparkling stars, seemed to go on forever.

Chapter Twenty-Three
Country Club Material

Georgia had opened her hope chest exactly twice this summer. Once: to retire her friendship bracelet. Twice: to take it *out* of retirement.

She'd retired the friendship bracelet because it had become a burden. Or, what was the metaphor Mr. Lowry had nailed into their heads after they'd read that poem, *The Rime of the Ancient Mariner,* by Samuel Taylor Coleridge? An albatross around her neck. The friendship bracelet had become precisely that — an albatross, an anchor that prevented her from doing new things. From being her own person.

Not to be overly dramatic, but Valerie had set her free.

The problem was that she hadn't imagined that there would be any cost. Stupidly, she hadn't really imagined that she'd *miss* Brooke and Charlotte. But she did. A lot. A month ago, she couldn't picture anything sweeter than replacing the worn bit of thread with something else: a thin gold chain, a silver tennis bracelet — or nothing at all. But now, after the blowup with her friends on the golf course, she wanted to reconnect with them in some small way. Putting the bracelet back on was part of that.

Downstairs, Mom and Dad were already puttering around the kitchen, brewing coffee and preparing eggs and toast. Georgia stared blearily at the other treasures inside the lacquered wooden box: a mottled Darien County Fair ticket stub, a tennis ball signed by Venus Williams (Brooke's present to Georgia on her sixteenth birthday), a bunch of juicy notes passed in class at the Tombs . . . all connected in some way to Brooke and Charlotte.

"Honey?" her mom called from downstairs. "Breakfast is ready!"

"In a sec, Mom," Georgia called back, her voice husky.

"You don't want to be late!" Mom shouted.

Georgia slammed the lid shut, squeezing the friendship bracelet in her hand. "Late for what?" she shouted back.

"For shopping! For the ball! Isn't today your shopping day?"

Oh, my God. Georgia had completely forgotten. For the past five summers, on the morning of the Midsummer Ball, she and Brooke and Charlotte had spent the entire day at the Old Fairfield mall, scouring the racks for slinky-sheer-shiny dresses for that evening. She'd assumed they *wouldn't* be going together this year.

Ding-Dong.

Georgia's hopes soared. The doorbell at this hour could mean only one thing: Charlotte or Brooke had come over to apologize.

"I'll get it!" Georgia yelled, bounding out of her bedroom and hurtling down the stairs. She nearly slipped in the front hallway; she was wearing her socks and pajamas. She raced forward and threw open the door —

"Hey, G."

Oh.

It was neither Brooke nor Charlotte. It was Ethan.

There he was, the model Silver Oaks employee. He'd shaved, and gotten a haircut. His crisp whites looked brand-new. And standing there before her at her front door (and what the hell even gave him the audacity to show up here at 9 A.M. on a Saturday?), he was almost a vision out of the past. He looked the way he'd looked when he'd *first* showed up at Silver Oaks, two summers ago, the summer before they'd gotten together — the summer when they'd merely played tennis and flirted, setting the stage for what would come later.

Something in Georgia snapped. She didn't offer a hello, or even a screw-you. She simply lunged forward and seized Ethan's polo pocket — with the freshly stitched *S.O.* silver monogram — and tore it clean off his shirt.

"Hey!" he cried, laughing and staggering backward.

Georgia hurled the pocket to the ground and thrust a shaky finger toward the end of Meadow Lane. "I want you to get out of here!"

Ethan glanced down at his ruined uniform, then back up at her. The smile never left his face.

"What are you so goddamned happy about?" Georgia demanded, putting her hands on her hip.

"Well, lots, actually. That's why —"

She stepped outside and slammed the front door behind her so her parents wouldn't hear.

"What were you thinking, trying to set me up with Caleb?" she whispered furiously. "Did you really think I'd have *sex* with him? Is that what you honestly thought?"

Ethan froze. "Wait, what?"

"You heard me."

Ethan's face turned ashen. "What on earth gave you that idea?"

"Valerie told me all about it. She told me that she heard you making a bet with Caleb that he could probably sleep with me if he just —"

"Slow down," Ethan whispered. "Slow down, okay? What kind of bet? What exactly did Valerie overhear?"

"She said that you told Caleb to invite me to the Midsummer Ball because you figured he could . . . get lucky with me."

The faint beginnings of another smile appeared at the corners of Ethan's mouth. His eyebrows mashed together in that cute way they always did when he was confused. "When? Was this in the parlor? The day you guys played golf? It was, wasn't it?"

"I don't know," Georgia muttered, suddenly out of steam. "Maybe."

"Ha!" Ethan grinned. "I knew she looked funny when she asked Caleb for the —"

"So what are you trying to tell me? You *never* made a bet with Caleb that he'd lose his virginity to me tonight?"

Ethan's mouth fell open. "Are you kidding? Is that what you think of me?"

Georgia shook her head. "I . . . I don't know, Ethan." Her voice caught on his name.

"G, the only reason I asked Caleb to invite you to the Midsummer Ball was because I couldn't stand the thought of you *not* going. I have to go — all employees do, remember? Or I did, until yesterday. And yes, I did say to Caleb: 'I bet you'll lose your virginity.' But I wasn't talking about *you*. I was talking about Charlotte. That kid is in *love* with Charlotte. And I thought . . . well, it's not something I'm proud of, but I thought I could help him out by making Charlotte jealous —"

"Wait," Georgia interrupted. "What do you mean, you did until yesterday?"

He grinned. "Oh, yeah. That's what I wanted to tell you. I quit."

"You *what*?"

He spread his arms. "You're looking at the newest part-time tennis coach at Old Fairfield Community College. I'm taking a year off from school. I'm no longer a student. I'm a teacher." He laughed. "You know what they say — if you can't do, teach."

Georgia's throat tightened. "Ethan, why?" she breathed shakily.

"Because I need a job, and because, well, I need to be with you. And this is the only solution." He stepped forward and took her hand. "G, the only reason I broke up with you was because of Silver Oaks. I applied for a job at Kenwood, and they turned me down —"

"They did?!" she cried. "Why didn't you tell me?"

"Because I didn't want you to feel sorry for me. And the truth is, I couldn't stand being away from you. So I kept staying at Silver Oaks." He drew her closer, squeezing her hand tighter. "But now this makes more sense. I never really was country club material, anyway, you know? I guess Kenwood picked up on that."

Georgia swallowed, her emotions whirling wildly. Her eyes fell to the torn pocket on the front walk, the *S.O.* glittering brightly in the morning sunlight, and she felt a stab of guilt. Her long blonde hair tumbled across her face. "But . . . but what about school? I mean, aren't you worried about taking time off?"

"It'll work out, G. If anything, this'll help. Maybe I can save enough to go somewhere even better than a community college."

"I . . . so . . . you never wanted to be friends at all, did you?" she stammered, afraid to even hope for his answer.

Ethan gently brushed a few strands of hair out of her eyes and met her gaze. "Of course I want to be friends," he whispered. "But I also want to be your boyfriend. That's all I've ever wanted. It's you, Georgia. It always has been, and it always has to be." He smiled. "And not just because you're the only girl who can beat me at tennis. Although that helps."

Suddenly, Georgia felt as if the entire weight of the universe had slipped away. All her silly doubts and fears that had plagued her all summer melted into nothingness.

But there was one lingering doubt.

"What about . . . you and *Valerie?*" Georgia whispered as Ethan came even closer and cupped her chin in his hands. "I — I saw you guys together, and Brooke told me —"

Ethan shook his head, frowning. "G, there was never any 'me and Valerie.' She's a fun, flirty girl, but there was nothing between us. Nothing at all. She just wants to make friends here."

Georgia nodded, her eyes filling with tears. So Ethan — and Valerie — *had* been faithful to her all along. "There's something I need to tell you," she blurted, her heart pounding. "I kissed Marcus. Just once. It was stupid and —"

Ethan shook his head. "G, you never were supposed to *wait* for me. It's okay. I'll live." He grinned. "Let's just focus on the future now, okay?"

Then he leaned in and kissed her, long and deep and sweet. Georgia twined her arms around his neck, breathing in that deliciously familiar aftershave, and fell a little bit more in love with him. When they finally broke apart, they were both grinning.

"What's that you're holding?" Ethan whispered. He delicately spread her fingers.

Georgia glanced down at the friendship bracelet, sniffling. "It's our trio-of-backup-singers thing. See when the doorbell rang, I was hoping it was Brooke or Charlotte."

Ethan nodded. His face grew serious. "So you heard about all the craziness?"

"What do you mean?"

"You didn't hear about Charlotte's freakout?"

Uh-oh. "No. Well, she and I have been sort of incommunicado . . . which is —"

"She was uninvited to the ball," Ethan interrupted. "She showed up last night, drunk and barefoot and smoking. She stubbed a cigarette out in your mom's wine, actually. Then she took off all her clothes, and made out with Caleb in the pool."

Georgia sagged against the front door. The sudden joy she had felt began to flow out of her, as if she were a tire pricked with a nail. "Oh, my God," she said finally.

"It sucks," he finally said. "But do you still want to go to the ball?"

Georgia closed her eyes. "I'd love to go. I mean: I'd love to go with *you*." She tapped a finger against her chin. "But if they're not inviting Charlotte, there's no way I'm gonna go." Her eyes opened and she sighed. "I can't believe Mom didn't even mention it."

Ethan gathered her in his arms. "Well, to be honest, I don't want to go, either."

"Hey, we'll have fun boycotting," she said, her breath tickling his neck. She rubbed his back and squeezed him tight. "My parents are going to the ball, obviously, so we'll have the house to ourselves. Maybe I'll even cook lasagna. I can even overcook it."

Ethan pulled back and blushed, looking very optimistic.

Georgia kissed him on the cheek, feeling hopeful — honestly *hopeful* — for the first time since last summer. "But hang on, okay? There are a bunch of calls I need to make before tonight. Starting with Charlotte."

Chapter Twenty-Four
Old Times

The good news was that nobody from Silver Oaks had called the von Klaus residence yet to complain about Charlotte's performance last night. (She preferred the word "performance" to "near-complete mental breakdown.") Maybe Mr. Farnsworth and the rest of the board figured they could rely on the old axiom: Ignore something unpleasant and it will go away. If they simply pretended Charlotte didn't exist, why would she want to hang out at their club anymore?

The bad news was that Mom caught her making out with Caleb in front of the house when he'd dropped her off.

Mom had given Charlotte the typical song-and-dance about how men weren't to be trusted, but Charlotte had tuned her out. She didn't want anything to ruin what she'd shared with Caleb — that unforgettable moment of connection in the pool, and then the ride home, during which they'd held hands and told each other all the truths they'd pretended weren't there for all those years.

Now, the next morning, Charlotte lay in bed, staring dreamily at the ceiling. Her mom had gone to the club to "patch things up." Charlotte didn't want things patched.

She snatched up her cell and dialed the only person she wanted in that moment.

"Hello?" Caleb answered. "C?"

"Hey there, stallion."

"I can't tell you how glad I am to hear your voice. Can I call you right back?"

Charlotte giggled. "You're *that* glad, huh?"

"Don't ask," he moaned. "I'm in the middle of a fight with my parents about going to the stupid freaking ball tonight, which I have no intention of doing, but —"

BEEP.

"That's my other line," Charlotte said. "Call me or I'll call you." She clicked the flash button. Her breath quickened when she saw the ID. It was Georgia. "Hello?"

"Hey," Georgia said quietly.

"Hey, yourself."

Georgia paused. "All right. There's a lot I want to say right now, but I think it's best if I just do it in person. I heard about what happened last night."

"You mean, that I almost had sex with Caleb Ramsey in the pool?"

"You *what*?"

"Yeah. It was pretty wild."

Georgia was quiet for a second. "I — I mean, I heard you guys kissed, but —"

"I'm kidding, G," Charlotte said dryly. She leaned back in bed and scratched Stella McCartney's belly. All of a sudden, she realized she was still wearing her Birkenstocks.

She hadn't changed out of them after walking Stella this morning. She hadn't been thinking about her shoes. She'd only been thinking of Caleb. *Yikes.* Was this what it meant to be in love?

"Listen, C, can I come over?"

Charlotte shrugged, baffled. *We get in the worst fight of our lives, and now you want to come over?* "Uh . . . well . . ."

"Well, you don't have much of a choice, I'm afraid. I'm in your driveway."

"You are?" Charlotte jumped out of bed and hurried over to her window, parting the curtains with one hand. She nearly laughed. There was Georgia, all right — waving from the driver's seat of her SUV. She was wearing the same outfit she'd worn when Charlotte and Brooke had found her in the rain at the state park on the Fourth of July . . . only there was one crucial difference.

This time, she was also wearing the ratty Darien County Fair bracelet. It dangled from her wrist as she waved.

Charlotte wasn't even sure how she felt. But maybe it was best not to feel. Maybe it was best just to *act*. She threw down her phone and hurried downstairs, opening the door.

Georgia stood on the front stoop. Her straight blonde hair hung in a narrow part over most of her face.

Charlotte nodded toward the friendship bracelet on Georgia's wrist. "What's with that?"

Georgia shrugged. "Nothing. I just felt sort of naked without it."

"Oh," Charlotte said. Her lips quivered. She wiped her eyes and bungled an attempt at a laugh. "Well, I know all about feeling naked."

"Yeah. I heard."

The two girls started laughing at the same time, and then Georgia took a step forward and wrapped her arms around Charlotte, who was already hugging her back.

"Is this totally cheesy?" Charlotte whispered, squeezing Georgia tight.

"If so, I'm dealing with it." Georgia laughed, sniffling. Charlotte peered over Georgia's shoulder. A car was pulling into the driveway: a green Jaguar. Brooke's dad's car. The car he lent to Brooke only on special occasions. Georgia and Charlotte broke apart, staring. The driver's side door slammed, and Brooke hopped out — stylishly but casually dressed in jeans and a tank top, made-up, and carrying her purse. She eyed Georgia, then smiled at Charlotte.

"Come on, C," she announced. "We're going shopping."

"Uh . . . we are?" Charlotte asked, her eyes darting between Georgia and Brooke.

"Yes. We are. Not for the Midsummer Ball, though. I'm boycotting it if you can't come. But the pre-ball shopping expedition is a tradition, and I'm not going to break tradition. This time, we're going shopping for *ourselves*." She hesitated in the driveway, very deliberately ignoring Georgia. "So are you in, or out?"

Charlotte didn't answer. She glanced at Georgia again.

Georgia stepped toward Brooke. "B, let me —"

"I was talking to Charlotte," Brooke interrupted.

"Brooke, I don't like Marcus," Georgia blurted.

Brooke scowled at her. "So why did you *kiss* him?"

"I wish I never had," she said with a heavy sigh. "And I have to be honest with you. He is amazingly gorgeous, and I was going through a hard time . . . but . . ."

"But what?"

"But he's not the *one*. Look . . . Don't get mad, all right?"

Brooke placed her hands on her hips. "G, it would be hard for me to get any madder than I already am."

"I don't think he's the one for *you*, either," Georgia said quietly. "You deserve better. He's a total player. He capitalizes on his looks. You shouldn't rush into something just because he's hot. Not to mention the fact that he's an employee. . . ." She grinned sadly. "I know. Pot calling the kettle black and all."

Brooke didn't answer.

Charlotte held her breath. *Come on, B,* she pleaded silently. *Stop being so stubborn. People break rules all the time. . . .* Her hopes rose. She could see that Brooke was staring at Georgia's friendship bracelet, and that her face was starting to soften.

Nobody said a word.

"Actually, the real question is, who uses the word 'capitalizes' in casual conversation?" Charlotte pointed out, just to break the silence.

Georgia laughed.

"What's so funny?" Brooke demanded, pursing her lips.

"We are," Charlotte said. "Look, B. Georgia just gave me a hug, and I highly suggest *you* give *her* a hug. You're the power nexus. The ringleader. You are the Tina Turner to our . . . whoever the other two singers were."

Finally, Brooke cracked a smile.

Georgia extended her arms, her friendship bracelet hanging from her left wrist. "B, I swear to you. . . . Actually, I want to swear to both of you." Georgia stepped forward. "I'm so sorry."

Brooke nodded thoughtfully. She flicked a stray strand of jet-black hair out of her face. "G, even if I accept your apology, what about Valerie? She's hit on pretty much every boy at Silver Oaks except Robby Miller."

Georgia nodded. "Yeah. I know. I was pissed at her, too, about Ethan. But I think I get her now. She really just wanted to make friends with people."

"To say the least," Brooke said, but she smiled again. She turned to Charlotte. "The real question is, what are we going to do about *you*?"

Charlotte shuffled forward in her Birkenstocks, squinting in the morning sunshine. Stella shambled out the door beside her. "You're going to the ball," she said. "Both of you."

"Are you nuts?" Brooke and Georgia asked at the same time.

"Jinx!" Charlotte cried.

They rolled their eyes simultaneously. Charlotte allowed herself a grin.

"Hey, how about we figure this out over some food?"

Georgia said. "Wanna go into town for shopping and brunch?"

Brooke shrugged. "Fine. But I still have to figure out what to do about Marcus. He asked me to the ball."

Georgia shrugged, too. "Great," she said. "All the more reason to come up with a plan."

And as the three girls regarded one another, all of them half smiling, none could deny that things between them were feeling suspiciously back to normal.

Chapter Twenty-Five

A Midsummer's Night Nightmare

The Midsummer Ball was everything Caleb had expected, and more. Meaning: It was the exact same fiasco Silver Oaks had thrown last year.

Hello, people? First: A Midsummer Night does not fall in August. Second: Festooning the dining room with cheesy streamers and magical fairy dust, and having people dress up in silly gowns and tuxes, does not make for a romantic evening. Well, maybe it does, but not if your new girlfriend is uninvited.

To make matters worse, Jimmy and the rest of the staff were serving the crab cakes and mushroom puffs while dressed in feathered caps, kilts, and ruffled shirts — Shakespearean garb. It was too painful. Caleb wondered why he'd even agreed to come to this travesty.

Then he remembered. His parents had forced him.

And it wasn't as if he could have said no, because A) he didn't have the *cajones* and B) Charlotte had insisted that he go — even though that pissed him off to no end. It was accepting defeat. It was tacitly saying, "Yes, C, I'll go to this stupid induction ceremony to which *you* aren't invited, even though you're the only reason I bother coming to this club every single day, anyway." But she promised him that she'd see him later. And there was a note in her voice, a suggestive tone he'd never heard before, that made him think something he probably shouldn't have, but couldn't help it. . . .

Maybe tonight will be the night.

It was supposed to be the night, anyway. At least that's what he'd always envisioned. He and Charlotte were supposed to have been swept up in that same Shakespearean magic all the grown-ups allowed themselves to be swept up in — and then he would take her home and make passionate love to her. But instead he was stuck here. Alone. Not only wasn't it magical, but it was cheesy and excruciating and went on and on.

Part I: The Toasts

Here, under the direction of their Fearless Leader, Mr. Farnsworth, everyone gathered in a semicircle around the inductees and raised their glasses. Then came the barrage. "When Caleb was four, I remember his favorite outfit was a little sailor's uniform." . . . [Cue laugh track] . . . "Do you remember the very first time Brooke carried a purse?" . . . [Cue laugh track again] . . . Both Caleb and Brooke were required to keep their glasses raised the entire time. Caleb thought his arm would fall off. He'd also stopped listening. He couldn't help but think of Ethan's term: "Dinosaurs." Yes, the dinosaurs had gathered, an extinct species, ostensibly to celebrate their heirs, those who would inherit the Silver Oaks mantle — but the funniest part was, only half of those scions had showed up: he and Brooke.

Charlotte: Uninvited. Georgia: Canceled.

Part II: The Pledge

As if the toasts weren't bad enough, Caleb and Brooke were then forced to make the Silver Oaks pledge. That would be even *more* painful if it weren't so pathetic. Yes, they actually had to place their hands on a Bible (a Bible!) and repeat word-for-word the eighty-plus-year-old vow as intoned by Mr. Farnsworth: *"I (State My Name) do solemnly swear to uphold all the rules and regulations of Silver Oaks and to preserve the spirit of the club in all areas of my life, on or off the premises."* Caleb was not a drinker, but he did solemnly swear that he'd never needed a glass of spiked punch more.

Part III: The Gauntlet

Upon the raucous cheer that followed the pledge, the Silver Oaks members formed two lines — one male, and one female — and Caleb and Brooke, duty-bound, passed down each line and shook every member's hand, accepting congratulations upon being made a member. Fortunately, Caleb could drain his champagne during this part. And then it was over.

* * *

Caleb loosened his tie and slouched back against the bar, sipping his third punch. Truly, booze *was* the only perk. When you were made a member, they let you indulge and imbibe. (Wink, wink!) He glared across the dining room. They'd cleared the tables to allow his parents and the rest of the members to mix and mingle, glasses clinking, chattering emptily.

At least he'd canceled his date with Valerie. (Or he'd left her a voice mail to that effect.) He should have followed Brooke's lead. As soon as the ritual had reached its conclusion, she'd scooted off to the basement. Who could blame her? She'd come to Silver Oaks tonight against her will, too, and for the exact reason he had: She couldn't say no to her parents.

And speaking of Brooke . . .

Marcus had arrived. He was straight out of *GQ* tonight — pin-striped, three-piece suit, blond hair slicked back . . . and unlike Caleb, a properly knotted tie.

"What's up, man," Marcus said, eyeing the punch bowl. "Congratulations."

"For what?"

"For being inducted as an official member."

Caleb burst out laughing, and nearly slipped off the bar. *Hmm.* Maybe he was a little buzzed. "Oh. Well. Thanks."

"So have you seen Brooke?" Marcus asked.

Caleb took a sip of punch, reigniting the pleasant fire in his belly. "Nope. Can't say that I have, Marcus."

"I know she's here. . . ." Marcus turned and searched

the room. "I guess she was pretty pissed about the whole Georgia thing."

Caleb shrugged. "The Georgia thing?"

"Yeah. You didn't hear?"

"About what?"

"That Georgia and I . . . you know, got together."

Caleb shook his head. "'Got together' might be pushing it there, Marcus."

Marcus spun back around, his eyes blazing. "What's that supposed to mean?"

"Well, I talked to Charlotte today. Pretty much all day. And I heard that you tried to kiss Georgia, even though you've been sneaking down to the downstairs sauna with Brooke for the past month. Which is cool, bro . . . I mean — I don't blame you. As Robe Miller might say, we got mad honeys up in this piece."

"*Robe* Miller?"

Caleb upended his glass. "Inside joke. Forget it."

"Yeah, well, luckily I won't have to try to figure out any of your inside jokes anymore," Marcus muttered. "I gave notice today."

"*What?*" Caleb asked, genuinely taken aback. He'd assumed Marcus would take a swing at him, not make a confession.

"My dad enrolled me in this intensive college prep course. My grades kind of suck, so I need to get it together for next year, you know?"

Caleb nodded. For a moment, he almost felt sorry for

the guy. "Well . . . uh, you can always hang out here as a guest," he offered clumsily.

"Yeah. Right." Marcus scoped out the room once more.

Some emo-rock song began to blare from the speakers set up around the room, and a rapid hush fell over the crowd. After the initial cringing, however, they went right back to mixing and mingling.

"So you haven't seen Brooke, huh?" Marcus asked. "I want to go look for her. Anything to get away from here . . ."

"I hear you, bro." Caleb smiled, watching him hurry out the patio doors. It took a moment for him to recognize the song — it was that band Bright Eyes. Classic! The powers-that-be undoubtedly assumed that Caleb would enjoy it. He looked like that lead singer guy (or so some said). Sure, even though none of his friends were here, just slap on some of that self-pitying music that all the kids love, and Caleb Ramsey would cheer up! Yet the timing couldn't have been more perfect, because he'd had this very conversation with Charlotte over the phone today, about how much they *both* hated emo.

I'm going to kill you for making me come here tonight, C, Caleb swore to himself. *And after that, well . . .* He smiled to himself.

His mind wandered back to the Midsummer Ball last year, when the last batch of heirs had been inducted. He remembered how bored and pissed off they'd looked, and how quickly they'd left. Well, now he could relate. What a freaking crock this whole thing was! His eyes settled on Mr. Farnsworth, as he held court over a small circle of women: Mrs. Farnsworth, Georgia's mom, Caleb's mom, Robby Miller's mom . . . so suave and debonair . . . and only when Mr. Farnsworth returned Caleb's unsteady gaze did the sparkle fade from his eyes.

Mr. Farnsworth excused himself and headed toward Caleb. "Congratulations again, Caleb," he said, extending his hand. "Welcome to Silver Oaks, officially."

Caleb shrugged, offering the weakest handshake possible.

"Maybe you ought to lay off the punch a little," Mr. Farnsworth added.

"Why?" Caleb raised a fresh cup to his lips. "Did you spike it?"

Mr. Farnsworth's face darkened. "Caleb, you know that was a foolish prank I pulled when I was young."

Caleb arched an eyebrow at him. "Sounds like what Charlotte pulled last night."

Mr. Farnsworth's eyes turned into two black stones. "This is an important evening for you, Caleb. Do you want me to talk to your parents?"

Caleb shook his head. "Not really. I'm just saying: If you can admit to being foolish when you were young, maybe you could cut Charlotte a little slack, too."

"Caleb, you clearly care about her, and I appreciate that. But let's face it, the girl has sought professional help, so we know she's unstable."

"Are you nuts?" Caleb hissed. A few heads turned, but

Caleb went on. "What planet do you live on? Who *doesn't* see a shrink these days? If anything, it's a sign that she's more stable than most."

Mr. Farnsworth smiled implacably. "Spin it however you want, Caleb."

"Spin it? You want spin? Her great-grandfather founded this freaking place with *your* grandfather. And she's closer with your daughter than you'll ever . . . you'll ever . . ." Unfortunately, he lost track of where he was going with that argument.

"Pardon?" Mr. Farnsworth's lip curled in a sneer. "Caleb, you're not making any sense. I really do think you've had quite enough to drink."

Before Caleb could say another word, Mr. Farnsworth filled his own cup with punch, then strolled away, his face breaking into a wide smile as some new guests arrived: the Packwood family. Truly, the Packwoods were a sight to behold. Valerie's mom was even taller than Valerie, and just as beautiful, her blonde hair cut stylishly short. And her father looked like a professional athlete. So did her brother. *Look at them,* Caleb fumed. *Smiling and shaking hands . . . uh-oh.*

For some reason, Valerie was hurrying straight toward Caleb.

"Hey," he gulped. "Sorry I canceled our date, but I just figured —"

"Caleb, can I talk to you for a second?" she interrupted. She turned back toward her family, still bunched together at the dining room entrance, surrounding Mr.

Farnsworth. "Here, come with me." She took his arm and steered him toward the patio doors, pushing through out into the warm night air.

"What's up?" he asked, struggling to remain steady.

"I think I made a big mistake," she murmured.

"What? By asking me to the ball tonight?"

She frowned and shook her head.

"So . . . what, then? By telling Georgia I made that bet with Ethan?" He smiled and slugged another gulp of punch.

Valerie brought a hand to her forehead. "Well, yeah, *that*," she mumbled. "And a bunch of other things, too."

"Did you want to hook up with Ethan?" Caleb asked. "Because I know someone who might have a problem with that —"

"No!" she hissed. "The only reason I've been talking to Ethan was because I thought he was trying to screw over Georgia." She sighed and stamped her foot. "It was a total misunderstanding! I'm not interested in Ethan. I'm not interested in anybody here! Not that way, at least. Um, no offense. See, Georgia called me this morning. And we talked. And after what she told me . . . I know I should have just kept my mouth shut. The last thing I wanted was to mess everything up between all you guys. I don't even really know any of you. But I *like* you, all of you . . . and I guess that's sort of the point. I wanted to fit in here, and I took it upon myself —"

"Valerie?" Caleb interrupted. He slurred the word slightly. It sounded more like *Val-wee*.

"Yeah?"

"You're rambling. But that's okay. I ramble, too. Anyway, I forgive you. And I get it. You don't want to screw any of us. In any way, literally or otherwise."

Valerie chewed her lip, shaking her head. "But I feel like in some way all our misunderstandings led to Charlotte's freakout."

"I agree." Caleb frowned.

"So that's why we're doing something about it," Valerie said, raising her eyebrows.

Caleb grinned, swaying on his feet. In spite of his drunkenness, he felt increasingly sober. Even energized. "Who's doing what?"

"There's a plan afoot. Charlotte didn't tell you because she knew you'd bag coming here if you knew about it. But you need to help me out." She scooted into the shadows by the cabana entrance and started digging through her shiny clutch. "You have a cell phone, don't you?"

Caleb nodded. "I do. But just so you know, I'm a little wasted."

Chapter Twenty-Six

Rescue

Brooke was in the basement, but, for once, she was not in the sauna. She was not French-kissing Marcus Craft (in fact, she'd spied him upstairs post-initiation but had specifically avoided him). She wasn't doing much of anything at all, other than standing in front of the lone Ping-Pong table in the corner, absentmindedly tapping one white ball with the paddle.

What am I doing here?

If only she hadn't listened to Georgia and Charlotte. The only reason she'd even agreed to come to this idiotic ball was that the two of them had made her swear she would come. And where the hell *were* they, anyway? Weren't they supposed to be getting in touch soon with some sort of plan in place? The three of them had gone out for a long, leisurely brunch at IHOP, and then headed to the mall where Brooke had picked up the flowy, pink Galaxy evening gown and strappy C Label heels she now wore. She'd been reluctant to say good-bye to the girls after that — because she'd missed their down-and-dirty planning, and because, for the first time all summer, things between the three of them felt *almost* like old times.

Brooke sighed and rested her elbows on the green Ping-Pong table. The Marcus–Georgia thing still upset her. But she was more heartbroken about the *idea* of Marcus. Her lifeguard fantasy had fallen flat. And to make matters worse, Charlotte and Georgia had somehow, through all the craziness of the summer, found their soul mates and fallen in love. Brooke swallowed hard, feeling a stab of envy and wondering if she would *ever* experience that certainty with a guy.

She heard footsteps and a railing creak at the top of the stairs.

Brooke frowned. She tossed her paddle aside and rushed across the room, her heels clicking on the concrete. It had to be her dad, pissed at her because she'd snuck away mid-party.

"*Psst!* Brooke! Come up! Now!"

Holy — It wasn't her father. Brooke's heart leaped. It was *Georgia*, wearing her Juicy tank, capris, and flip-flops. Brooke lifted the ends of her skirt and clattered up the stairs. Georgia seized her wrist before Brooke even reached the top, her fingers tightening around Brooke's friendship bracelet — and then she started sprinting down the hallway toward the main entrance. Brooke kept up as best she could, her heels skidding and sliding as they rushed past the parlor and billiards room.

Georgia pushed open the front doors. Her SUV was waiting in the driveway, the engine running. Valerie sat in the passenger seat — her hair flowing over her shoulders, dressed in a strapless red dress. She flashed a quick smile and opened the back door for Brooke, ushering her into the back.

"Come on!" Valerie hissed as Georgia clambered into the driver's seat.

Georgia slammed her foot on the accelerator, throwing Brooke against the upholstery as she closed the door. Part of Brooke wanted to laugh; part of her wanted to dive out on the front lawn as Georgia swerved off the driveway and plowed through the grass to avoid the speed bumps. *Jesus!* Brooke spun in the seat, staring out the back window at the ugly tire tracks Georgia had torn in the golf-green-like expanse. A million questions raced through her mind, but for some reason, the very first one that popped out of her mouth was: "What about Marcus?"

"Don't worry," Georgia said, screeching out onto the public road. "He's not invited."

Brooke gripped the door handle. "Uh . . . not invited to what —"

"Georgia's throwing a party," Valerie said. "And you're the guest of honor. Well, one of the guests of honor."

"Actually, the *second* guest of honor," Georgia said. "No offense, B. Charlotte's the real guest of honor. She's already there. Caleb rounded up Robby Miller and Mike and Johnny and Billy, too. So it'll be a real party."

Brooke fumbled with her seat belt, trying to organize her thoughts. "A real party?"

"Yeah," Georgia said. "A *real* Midsummer Ball. But I wanted it to be a surprise. For you, I mean. That's why we had to kidnap you."

"I . . ." Brooke was still at a loss.

"It was partially Valerie's idea," Georgia added. She jerked to a stop at a red light.

Brooke nearly choked as she lurched forward. "You guys, I don't mean to be an alarmist here, but this strikes me as kind of strange. . . ."

"It's an apology," Valerie explained.

"Huh?"

Valerie peered over the edge of the passenger seat. "It's an apology for the way I acted. Like, all summer I was just . . . nervous. And so I kind of overcompensated."

"Overcompensated for what?"

"For how I have to start over in this new place and all that. . . ."

Brooke shook her head. "Valerie, maybe *I'm* the one who owes you an apology." She couldn't believe she was saying these words, but for the first time all summer, she felt clear-headed.

"Why?"

"For shutting you out." Brooke stared at the dark road ahead, fiddling with the hem of her skirt. "For being so cliquey, so exclusive. I can be that way sometimes."

Valerie cleared her throat. "It's okay."

"But I do have a question," Brooke continued. "It's the same question I asked Georgia. *Do* you want Marcus? Or Ethan? Or Caleb?"

"*What?*" Valerie laughed. She quickly clamped a hand over her mouth. "I mean, they're all cute. . . . Hmm. That came out wrong. Short answer: No."

Brooke grinned. "What's the long answer?"

"The long answer is, I just moved here," Valerie finished. "My grades suck, and I need to get my act together. . . . And — well, as you can see, I'm more interested in making new friends than in actually dealing with all my issues. And to be honest, all my old friends were scheming and conniving. That's why they dropped me so fast. And that's also probably why I used their same tactics here. . . . It's sort of all I know. Once my so-called friends found out I couldn't belong at our old school, they didn't let me belong with *them*." She peered around the seat. "That said; it *is* summer. School is out. So I say we just have fun tonight, okay? Because there's somebody I want you to meet."

"Who's that?"

Georgia smiled at Brooke in the rearview mirror. "Her brother, Sebastian."

Sometimes, it was best just to let emotions and baggage fall by the wayside — even if only for a little bit. Valerie was right; it *was* summer. So when Georgia pulled up to her house on Meadow Lane, and the three of them strode out into the backyard and Brooke saw the scene out by the pool . . . well, she decided to forget about worrying.

True, the Palmers would be home in a few hours. But this was the real Midsummer Ball, as it should have been. It was a big old mess, but everyone was here, as promised. Crumpled cups and bags of chips were scattered everywhere. Robby Miller and his crew were swimming with Ethan. Caleb was dozing in a lounger next to the bushes, still suited up in his tie and blazer. Charlotte sat in her bikini and sarong on a chair right next to the diving board, a drowsy smile on her face — though occasionally, she cast a longing glance toward Caleb.

Brooke sighed contentedly. She yanked off her heels and took a seat on the chair next to Charlotte. Georgia took the chair beside Brooke. Ethan leaped out of the pool and planted himself squarely on Georgia's lap, splashing all of them.

"Hey, watch it!" Brooke cried, but she didn't feel truly annoyed.

"Ah . . . you're used to it, pool girl," Georgia teased.

A thought occurred to Brooke as she surveyed the increasingly chaotic scene in the water: It was the first time she'd seen any of the pool boys actually *in* a pool.

"You know, G," Brooke began as Georgia and Ethan started kissing. "I really don't . . ." Her voice trailed off.

Valerie reappeared, followed by a very tall, very handsome, curly-haired blond guy. He had deep-set blue eyes that crinkled up when he smiled. The best part about him, even in the dim backyard light, was his clothing: hip, but not *too* hip — a T-shirt with a skeletal fish logo and the words "Flying Spaghetti Monster," and frayed jeans. In other words, he didn't look like the kind of guy who spent a whole lot of time in front of the mirror every morning. (Unlike, say, Marcus Craft.) Which, to Brooke, was very, very refreshing.

"This is my brother, Sebastian," Valerie said to Brooke.

Brooke shook his hand. "Nice to meet you, Sebastian."

"Likewise."

Valerie hurried away.

Sebastian smiled shyly, glancing at his sister over his shoulder. "So apparently, we should get to know each other," he said, turning toward Brooke again.

Brooke giggled. "Why's that?"

"I'm not really sure. I think because you like the Strokes."

"Actually, I don't really like the Strokes anymore," she shot back.

"Neither do I," he said dryly. "I just put that on my MySpace profile."

Brooke arched an eyebrow. "You have a MySpace profile?" *She* had one but didn't know many guys who did.

"No. Well, not yet. But, if I did, I would say that I prefer the Hives."

Brooke bit her lip, blushing. "Hmm. Good taste in music. A rarity among boys."

"Thanks," he said. "And who knows — maybe there's even more we have in common."

Now Brooke was certain that her face was bright red. Good thing it was so dark out. She nodded. "Maybe," she managed.

"It's like the great Nick Hornby says," Sebastian remarked. "It's not what you're like, it's what you *like*. So maybe my sister wasn't so far off the mark. You know, about how you and I should meet."

Brooke lowered her eyes. That was pretty damn true,

wasn't it? After all, Marcus was *like* a J. Crew model. But as far as any shared interests (aside from making out, but that didn't count) . . . there wasn't a whole lot there. In about forty-five seconds though, Sebastian Packwood had managed to establish a deeper connection.

"Well, let's not take this enlightening conversation *too* seriously," he joked. "Hey, I'm gonna get a beer. Want one?"

"Sure. Thanks."

"Okay." He smiled at her, holding her gaze. "So that makes two things we have in common. The Hives, and an appreciation for beer."

Before Brooke could say something foolish or embarrassing, Valerie reappeared. *Thank God.* She took her brother by the arm and steered him back toward Georgia's kitchen. Brooke didn't stop watching until he disappeared through the door.

"Uh-oh," Charlotte said in a singsong voice. "B's getting that look in her eye."

Georgia laughed. "Who wouldn't?" She giggled.

"Hey!" Ethan said, elbowing her. "Watch it, there."

"Kidding." Georgia kissed him on the cheek.

Brooke sighed happily, twirling her friendship bracelet around her wrist.

"What are you thinking, B?" Georgia asked.

"I'm thinking: Of *course* I'm getting that look in my eye," Brooke said. "We have three weeks left until school starts, you guys, and we'd better enjoy them. I told you this summer was going to be killer, didn't I?"

Epilogue: Summer Season Wrap-Up

The Silver Oaks Country Club
~ 195 NORTH ROUTE 37 ~
OLD FAIRFIELD, CT
06415

September 4

Dear Members,

Once again, the summer is drawing to a close. And what a summer it was!

In news: We were honored to induct Brooke Farnsworth and Caleb Ramsey as official members at our annual Midsummer Ball. After much deliberation, as well as an outpouring of support from other official members, we were also honored to induct Georgia Palmer and Charlotte von Klaus as members at a separate private ceremony the following week.

We welcome these four exceptional young people into our club, and trust they will uphold the values and traditions that have made Silver Oaks such a special family for over eighty years.

In other news: We were very sad to see our tennis instructor, Ethan Brennan, leave. He's taken a job at Old Fairfield Community College, but promises he'll still be a regular on the courts! We were also regretful to say good-bye to one of our lifeguards, Marcus Craft. But in happy news, Sebastian Packwood, the son of new members, has mentioned he might like to man the lifeguard chair next summer — so keep your eyes open! And as you have probably guessed, he and his sister, Valerie, are prime candidates for induction at next year's Midsummer Ball.

Here's to a happy and prosperous autumn.

Best,

The Silver Oaks Board

Three girls. One guy. This could get messy . . .

Don't miss

loud, fast, & out of control

BY NINA MALKIN

Available June 2006

Turn the page for a sneak peek!

(Woo-Hoo! of the Month . . .)

Who: 6X, a three-girl, one-guy, upbeat-yet-angsty pop-rock combo.

What: *Bliss de la Mess*, a mix of self-penned tunes and quirky-cool covers from the eighties and nineties. The sound? Come on, doesn't the album title tell all?

When: Last summer, when Angel Blue had that super-scary skateboarding accident, 6X stepped up to replace her band on the *Steal This Pony* soundtrack. (As if you didn't know!) Now their long-awaited debut disc is out, and first single "All Over Oliver" will have you doing the stiletto-heel stomp on that guy who had the nerve to break your heart.

Where: Band members (singer Kendall, 15; drummer Wynn, 15; bassist Stella, 16; and guitarist A/B, 17) all live in New York. But we expect they'll soon be calling a tour bus home!

Why: Because Kendall's a real role model who's not a toothpick! Because Stella's got attitude to burn! Because Wynn is a poet who makes perfect sense! Because A/B knows how to be just friends with girls . . . or does he . . . ?!

Now that I'm famous my cousin Carlene is on me like glaze on a roast ham. Last time I saw her, she acted all superior, her with her promise ring and her fiancé; now she's my best friend. Does she think my sparkle rubs off? I act real gracious as she shepherds me around, flaunting me. Thank goodness I brought plenty of press kit photos. A little gesture on my part — for the people of Frog Level, a treasure forever.

It's nice seeing everyone, having the whole town at my feet, but I'm distracted, disconnected. Lately, the whole idea of home is an itch I can't reach. Is home here in South Carolina, where I was born? Or up in New Jersey, at my mom's house? Or in my fabulous Teen Towers apartment, which I haven't been to once since we came off tour. I ought to be completely at ease down South, yet instead I feel more "on" than ever. In the East Village, with so many people — students and artists, professionals, bums, just everybody — you can be anonymous. Even if you're recognized, people show respect; they won't fawn all over you unless it's a die-hard fan about to wet his britches. Here, whether in the Piggly Wiggly or the Dairy Queen, people come over and talk to you like they have every right.

Well, I take that in stride, but I'm glad we're leaving soon. Not that I have any hoop-de-hoo New Year's plans. I know who I want to spend it with — I just can't figure out how to wrangle it, until Jane Marie Fulton starts gushing over my earrings.

"They're real unusual," she says, reaching out to touch them. We're all at the Dairy Queen, me and Carlene and her girlfriends. I pray Jesus will prevent Jane Marie from leaving greasy fingerprints on my most cherished Christmas present. "They sure don't have anything like them over at the Claire's."

Claire's! As if A/B would have bought my gift at some old chain store. "Thank you, Jane Marie." Semiprecious stones glitter and swing as I toss my head. Jane Marie's fingers retreat. "They were a gift from A/B."

"Really?" Jane Marie and Carlene and Devon are more interested now — they start asking all about A/B. It's like feeding fish in a pond; throw a couple of crumbs and they gobble them up. But I say, "Oh, I can't talk about that," so it gets through their cinder-block brains that it's rude to intrude. Still, I look kindly at Jane Marie — thanks to her a great idea occurs to me. "Tell you what, I can call A/B and find out where he got them," I say. "I'm sure it's some exclusive boutique, but maybe they take phone orders."

"Would you, Kendall?" Jane Marie lights up. "Wow, that would be so nice!"

I pat her hand. "I sure will," I say. Well, then they

all gawk at me like I'm going to call A/B right then and there! "Later . . ."

Only when will I get a moment's peace to do so? My grandparents' house is small, and me and my mom share what was her room growing up. What with the close quarters and all the company coming and going, it's not till eleven at night when my mom takes her shower. I slip out my cell.

"Heyyyy, Kendall."

Gosh, it's good to hear his voice! "Hey, A/B! Did you have a good Christmas? I sure hope so!"

"Cool, you know, your basic Jewish Christmas: a movie and Chinese food."

It always slips my mind that A/B is Jewish — another river to cross. "Well, mine was wonderful. One day, A/B, you'll have to experience a country Christmas. But look here, the reason I'm calling . . ." I get that out of the way, then progress, doodling hearts on my note-pad. "We're coming back the day after tomorrow. I've pretty much had my fill of Frog Level, but, well, things have been so hectic since the tour and rushing on down here and all, I haven't made a single plan for New Year's. Isn't that hilarious? Kendall Taylor with nothing to do on the biggest party night of the year."

I let it sink in a second. The thing with A/B is, if I set him up with the right signals and let him know it's okay for him to be forward, he does the right thing. Of course he does! That's why I love him so!

The Boy

Not only did I ask Edie out for New Year's two whopping months in advance, I told her we'd do whatever she wants. Whipped much? To my chagrin, she vetoes the Ramones tribute in favor of a Long Island house party. But wait, there's more. Apparently I deserve to be flogged for inviting one of my bandmates.

"A/B, how could you?!" Edie's not pleased to learn Kendall's our third wheel.

This baffles me. After all, Edie made no bones about the fact that she wants me at this party to cement her status in a new social stratum. Logically I assume the only thing more ingratiating than one rock star is two rock stars. "How could I what?"

Edie narrows green laser beams and performs heart surgery, sans anesthetic.

"It's not like we'll have to attend to her all night. People will be all over her, and Kendall loves that kind of attention. She's coming by car service; we won't have to chauffeur her around." Edie's mouth is a thin pink line. I switch gears, go for her soft spot. "Come on, the poor kid had nothing to do. How would you feel?"

Success!

"Why couldn't I have fallen for a cruel, heartless

bastard?" Edie asks the ceiling. "Why did I have to fall for a sweet mushy dumbass instead?"

I snatch her in my arms for a quick canoodle. "Too bad for you," I whisper into her clavicle. "Sweet mushy dumbass — forever."

The party, while hardly a history-making rock-and-roll event, is off to a pleasant start. Not nearly as jappy as I feared. Edie lives in a modest middle-class town, but the soiree's a few notches up on the utsy scale. Every house is on the water, a boat in every backyard. But the dozen or so kids already assembled are low-key and friendly. There's a slight haze of cheeba, and no keg. Hummus and baba ghanoush. Kings of Leon and Bob Marley. Basically, a well-to-do neo-hippie gathering. I fit in fine.

Our hostess, the olive-skinned, hook-nosed Santhea, is the new friend of Edie's BFF Alexa. There's been some shuffling of late — Edie met me, Alexa met Santhea — this is really the first chance for everyone to get acquainted. I don't know a soul besides Edie, but hey, several months of celebrity and the rigors of touring have made me at ease anywhere, except maybe a Taliban hideout.

There's no hint the party will go out of bounds. Santhea's tolerant parents are on premises, amiably monitoring — they don't actually hit off the bong, but there's no need to be surreptitious about it. We're not big drinkers — most of us sip mineral water or soda, although champagne, uncorked as of yet, is on ice. As New Year's anticipation grows with the crowd, the vibe stays mellow, copacetic.

Then Kendall makes her entrance. And everything changes.

Not in a big way, though. It's subtle. A shift as opposed to a swing. Six months ago Kendall would have been invisible to these people. Her "off-ness" would have gone unnoticed. Now her "off-ness" has become the "on-ness" of a rock diva. She walks in, her presence acknowledged with a buzzy effect.

Caftan flowing as she runs to the door, Santhea clasps Kendall's hands, takes her coat, leads her around. No introduction required. Everyone knows who she is.

Kendall doesn't beeline for Edie and me, standing near the fireplace, dipping pita triangles into Middle Eastern delights. She chats amiably with one cluster of admirers after another, her Southern accent sonic flower petals against the nasal "oh-my-gawds!" of Nassau County. Then she waves, weaves our way. Edie stiffens. For no reason. No reason at all. Except that's how it is. Edie does not want Kendall here. And that's that.

But Edie's a cool person; she doesn't want to be a bitch. Plus, she likes herself, so she hates feeling threatened. Who can she blame for her current state of affairs? That would be me. Right about then Kendall ambles over. "Hey, you guys! Happy Almost New Year!" The chummy three-way hug she goes for gets neatly cross-checked. "Oh, Edie," she says. "Your friends are all real nice."

"They're not my friends," Edie says flatly. "I don't even know these people."

"Oh? Really? I thought — well, they're awful nice."

Then she turns to me. "Hey, A/B! What's that you're munching on?"

"Ah, well, that's hummus — ground-up chickpeas. And baba ghanoush is — "

"Boboga . . . what?! Bless my soul!" Kendall swats my arm. "You're joshing me — that's not even a real word. Edie, he must keep you in stitches."

"Sure," she seethes. "Though sometimes I'd like to see him in stitches."

Silence. Awkward silence. The mother of all awkward silences. At least for me. It's possible Edie enjoys her fury on some perversely justified level. And Kendall, I doubt she picks up any nuance of weirdness.

"You know, A/B, I bet we're in the worst trouble with Mr. Wandweilder for skipping that Ramones thing," she blathers on. "Stella's the only one from the band going, as far as I know, but everyone who's anyone else is sure to be there."

"You said she had nothing else to do." Edie breathes the words at me.

Before I can begin to conjure an explanation, Kendall goes on: "Well, I reckon we can always go late if this party gets dull. I have the driver all night. Gosh, all the traffic was going the other way — smooth sailing coming out here. That driver could not believe I was leaving the city for Long Island."

That rips it for Edie. She ekes out an "excuse me" and bolts. I ought to go racing after her, but what would I say?

"Is she . . . all right?" Concern creases Kendall's face.

"She — she's mad at me," I manage, obliquely, lamely.

"Oh, gosh, A/B! It's not because I'm here, is it?"

The last thing I want is to make two women miserable! "No, Kendall. It's not you, it's me." Yep, those words actually come out of my mouth. "I'd better —"

"No, let me go. Girls know how to talk to each other." She touches my arm comfortingly. "Don't you worry, I'll just make chitchat, let her see how nice and regular I am. She doesn't know me the way you do."

Makes sense. If Kendall intimidates Edie, only Kendall can make it right. Right? Sure! By the stroke of midnight it will be worked out, canned sitcom laughter in the background. So I let Kendall follow Edie while I wander in search of that bong. Several heady hits later, I am feeling no pain. Cloud-walking, my head and feet turned to sponge. Those three guys I'm smoking with — Sam, Dan, and . . . Wham, is it? Spam . . . ? They've got some good shit and are ridiculously generous.

So when an extra oomph of excitement stirs the atmosphere, it takes me a while to figure out what's up. Santhea's a burbling blur, passing out noisemakers and hats; her parents pop champagne corks and fill plastic glasses. Dan, Sam, and Spam float toward dates like astronauts in zero gravity. Santhea slaps a paper cone on my head, snaps the elastic under my chin. This shouldn't be funny but it is.

The countdown begins: "Ten! . . . Nine ! . . . Eight ! . . ."

A whiff of perfume behind me . . .

"Seven! . . . Six! . . . Five! . . ."

A tender touch at my elbow . . .

"Four! . . . Three! . . . Two! . . ."

I turn woozily around.

"ONE!!!"

"Happy New Year, A/B!" The voice honey, the eyes stars.

"Happy New Year, Kendall . . ."

The room starts to spin. "Auld Lang Syne" kicks in. Kendall and I ring in the new year like any boy and girl who find themselves facing each other at midnight. With a kiss.

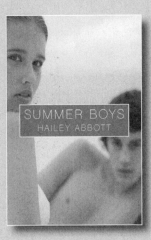